LOVE GONE WRONG

VOLUME 7

THE CASTLE OF HORROR ANTHOLOGY

CASTLE BRIDGE MEDIA
DENVER, COLORADO, USA

CASTLE BRIDGE MEDIA
Denver, Colorado
Edited by Jason Henderson and In Churl Yo
Designed by In Churl Yo
Cover Photo Bence Balla-Schottner/Unsplash

ISBN: 978-1-7364726-9-9

TABLE OF CONTENTS

INTRODUCTION

LOVE IS.

Full stop.

An argument can be made that love might best be left in the abstract, that in its purest form, love offers us far more as a positive ideal than it otherwise might in its derivative. It's only when we attempt to define love by inserting ourselves within this concept that it tends to falter and degrade, and things get messy and oh, so complicated. When passion gets added to the mix, things usually become even worse. Much, *much* worse.

For good or bad, love is an essential part of our existence, and often, when they say that life is suffering, the culprit behind that sentiment can be traced in some way to love. Whether unrequited, lost, true, self, or abused, love is our constant companion from the familial to the romantic, from our first faltering steps as toddlers all the way up to our very last. Even in its complete absence, love affects us in fundamental, yet often detrimental, ways.

But then, that's the point, isn't it? Despite how crazy or miserable it makes us, the sacrifices we choose to achieve love are all worth it in the end. That, as Huey Lewis would say, is the power of love. Love offers purpose and meaning. It completes us. It makes an otherwise dour and scary world almost bearable by making us feel safe. Alive. Accepted. *Loved.* Love does this freely without prejudice. For anyone who has ever been in love, you know this to be true.

And yet, a fine line also exists between love and insanity. For anyone who has ever thought they might have been in love but were dead wrong, you know this to be true as well.

Love can not only make us, but it can also make us do terrible, awful things in its name. This volume of the *Castle of Horror Anthology* seeks to walk that fine line, to expose the terror that love can sometimes leave in its wake, taking us on occasion into dark and scary places.

We offer you this rich assemblage of love-gone-wrong tales for your reading pleasure:

New York Times bestselling author Alethea Kontis brings us a solemn, black magic revenge yarn with *The Witch of Black Mountain.*

Writer extraordinaire P.J. Hoover discovers an old, abandoned house deep in the woods and the love that perished there in *Black Heart.*

Pulp Factory Award winner Teel James Glenn's *Black Sails* shows what happens when an artificial intelligence inserts itself into its user's relationship.

Lovecraft scholar Jeremiah Dylan Cook allows us to peer into the journals of a delusional patient and the mysterious, magical book that influences her relationship with his story *Seven Entries in the Midnight Path.*

Choices by the amazing Will McDermott reveals how a firefighter with a unique gift attempts to use it to save his marriage.

Lewis Figun Westbrook weaves a passionate, highly provocative tale where the figurative becomes literal in *A Love All Consuming.*

Bram Stoker Award® nominee Frazer Lee's *Ill Met by Moonlight* offers an intimate and heart-breaking take on a classic monster story.

By the Cold of the Moon weaves an Old-World tale of love, deception and immortality written by the astounding Liz Holliday.

Tom Waltz gives us a remarkable small-town, KISS-influenced, account of a seemingly typical high school Friday night, a beer run, and regret, in the charged *Love Gun.*

The Loneliness of Monsters by the incredible Scott Pearson reflects on

5

a mother's love for her son where in the end, not all is quite what it seems.

An Egyptian funeral bottle becomes the vessel through which jealousy and revenge blossom in Steven Philip Jones' marvelous *Expiration Date*.

And finally, Mike Owsley pens an uncanny Lovecraftian tale about a love between a painter and a writer, and the setting that binds them, in *The Wharf*.

Jason and I consider it a great privilege to share these wonderful stories of love gone wrong with you, showcasing a cadre of unique voices from the genre's best authors. Thank you always for supporting independent publishing, and please consider seeking out other volumes from the *Castle of Horror Anthology* series to enjoy even more outstanding tales of the eerie and the sublime.

We are sure you will *love* them all. ♜

–In Churl Yo, Publisher, Castle Bridge Media

THE WITCH OF BLACK MOUNTAIN

By Alethea Kontis

LETTING ANTHONY GENTRY GET HER pregnant was the stupidest thing Ennica Jamison had ever done. Hiking to the summit of Black Mountain to see a witch was the second. It had been a warm November afternoon when she'd left her stolen horse on the path at the base of the mountain; now it was cold and dusk. She placed a foot on the first step of the abandoned lookout tower. She'd been walking for hours, slow but determined, sprinkling what sanity she had left behind her like breadcrumbs in the dirt. She grasped the rusted orange railing firmly with a gloved hand. One last thing left to climb. One last moment before she discovered just how stupid she really was.

She stomped her boots hard on the metal to make sure there was no ice; each step brought one more inescapable thought along with it. Every time she closed her eyes, she saw herself stabbing Anthony in the heart—the heart he didn't have—so she tried not to close her eyes, but her mind still raced against her will. How he and that bitch Tanya must have laughed at her; how they must be laughing at her still. Her father would be mad that she'd taken the horse out overnight, but he'd be furious when he found out he was going to be a grandfather.

It didn't have to be a knife. Maybe a spear, like in the ancient days of

Spartans and honor. Anthony wouldn't have survived long in that world. The dream of his blood pooled in her hands, all his life and all his lies drained away. No. Concentrate on something else. One more step.

She was high enough now to see where the elevation benchmark disc lay, the official plaque set in stone by the Geodetic survey crew back in the fifties. She had passed it fifty yards or so back and wondered if she'd been kin to anyone on that team. Probably. Over four thousand feet up...and two more steps.

Her panting breath froze her tongue, the fog before her reminding her of the surreally beautiful ice on the rock face a mile or so back. If she was ever crazy enough to come back this way, she'd have to bring a camera. If she survived. Three more steps. The tower creaked and shivered. It might have been her shivering.

It had been a girl in the schoolyard who had told Ennica about the lookout tower. "But built to look out for *what*?" she'd asked rhetorically, chewing on the end of one of her ribboned chestnut plaits. "I'll tell you what. My nanna says if you climb to the top of that tower, it'll show you where the witch lives." The Witch of Black Mountain, the dark fairy long ago cast out of the magic circle. The one who grants wishes and eats babies and who'll come and suck your soul if you don't put your toys away before supper.

Supper. Ennica couldn't remember if she had stopped for supper. It didn't matter. One final step, and she was at the top. She looked out over the clearing, scanned the treetops.

A lone crow drifted in and out of the mist on the early evening currents. Other than that, she saw nothing.

Ennica took a deep breath, sucking in more cold than oxygen, and blew out another cloud of fog. She wasn't surprised; deep down she'd known this was a one-way trip. Supplies would have just slowed her down. Her whole body was tired. She just didn't have the strength to walk anymore. They'd find her huddled at the base of the tower, peacefully frozen in her sleep. Or perhaps she'd just stay right here up at the top, the closest she'd ever be to the stars in this life. Spiritual, almost.

A sob escaped her; her chest felt like a mason jar about to explode.

Her cry echoed over the quiescent landscape, unanswered by nightingale or Chuck Will's Widow or that ephemeral crow. Even the cicadas didn't dare infest this high. The night was a tomb. Fitting, really. She felt tears eke out and freeze on her lashes. She refused to be a wimp, especially if she was the only one around to witness it, so she blinked them away. *Blink.*

Anthony. Stabbed. Blood. Relief.

Ennica gasped and opened her eyes again. She wished she was brave enough to go through with something like that, brave enough to save the world from one more lying, cheating, thieving bastard. Hell, she couldn't even save herself. If she'd have lived through this, her kid would have been a bastard too. She didn't mind.

She put a hand on her still-flat belly. Hopefully it was warmer in there. Without closing her eyes, Ennica imagined she was sitting in front of a nice, warm fire. It smelled of cedar and coal and hand-me-down quilts. It blurred her vision and burned her eyes. She rubbed them, looking out over the mountaintop.

She wasn't dreaming.

Ennica followed the smoke trail back to its origin and could just barely make out the silhouette of a rooftop among the trees. She memorized its location in relation to the tower before scrambling down, snatching her pack up, and hightailing it to the front door. She pulled off her gloves; her skin was so dry when she rapped on the door that her knuckles bled.

"Yes?" the soft female voice was followed by the furious flapping of wings and the cackle of a crow.

"I'm looking for the w—" Ennica stopped herself. "Witch" didn't quite seem the polite term. "—the dark fairy," she finished.

"Fairies. Bah," said the woman. "Blanton Forest is about four leagues west. If you want romance, you're on the wrong mountain."

"Romance got me into this," Ennica called through the door. "Now all I want's revenge." There was no reply. Ennica counted her heartbeats: One. Two. Three. Four. Five. When she got to a hundred, she'd...she'd what, leave? She had nowhere to be. Here on this porch seemed as good a place to freeze to death as any.

She heard rattling, and then the door opened a crack. "Come in."

The cabin was small—only one room—with no furniture to speak of apart from a simple table and two chairs beside a squat black stove. Ennica fell to her knees before it, suddenly aware of how cold she was, and exactly how close to death she'd come already. The fire smelled of coal, wood smoke, apple pie, and lilacs. There. It was official; she'd lost her mind. But she'd suspected that the minute that low-down, dirty rotten liar had kissed her.

Lord bless the genius who one day invented the soap that could wash memories like that out of her mind.

"Sit," said the witch. She had taken one of the chairs at the table, the crow perched on her shoulder. Before the other chair sat a plain white teacup filled with water. Ennica pulled herself up into the chair and cradled the cup in her icy fingers.

"What's this?" she asked.

"Whatever you want it to be," said the witch. The crow agreed.

Ennica nodded and took a sip. What hit her tongue was not water but hot chocolate—not the weak, powdery stuff she'd drunk as a kid but honest-to-goodness cocoa, the thick, molten creaminess that rich people had for breakfast in all those books she liked to read. *See, baby?* she said to her womb. *This is what you deserve in life.* Not too bitter; not too sweet. It tasted elegant and beautiful, and as it coursed through her veins it calmed her nerves and warmed her bones, lulling her into a sense of comfort. She closed her eyes...

...and saw Anthony and Tanya, naked, passionately devouring one another. She mentally skewered them together with one thrust of her spear and shoved the vision aside. Damn them both. They were not going to ruin her chocolate.

Bravery reinforced, she opened her eyes. She'd doodled her fair share of witches on her notes in class; old and wizened and warty, sultry and buxom and irresistible. The woman stroking the silky coal-black feathers of the crow didn't look anything like them. She wasn't young or old. Her features and coloring were the averagest of average. She could have been any woman on the street. She could have been the clerk at the grocer's. For that matter, she could have been kin—she looked quite a bit like her cousin Jessica. Ennica sipped her magical chocolate again. "I'm Ennica," she said finally.

The witch raised her eyebrows. "Interesting."

"I was named after my grandmother, Eunice," Ennica explained. "The nurse who filled out the birth certificate had terrible handwriting." Her words sounded stupid even as she was saying them. *Nice, Ennica. Now maybe we can chat about the weather and our favorite music and try on each other's clothes.* "Are you really a witch?" *Oh, well done there, idiot.*

The witch smiled.

"Sorry. I'm just...I mean, I meant..."

"Don't apologize," said the witch. "So, few people ask the right question. For all your self-loathing, you're really quite perceptive."

Right. If she was so perceptive, she would have known that Anthony had never loved her.

"That's exactly what I'm talking about," said the witch, reading her mind. "Now cut it out and drink your chocolate."

She'd been raised to respect her elders...which she figured might as well include anybody who might have the power to turn water into chocolate. Ennica did as she was told.

"This is Mr. Hue," the witch introduced the crow, and it lowered its head to Ennica.

"Nice to meet you, Mr. Hue."

"To answer your question: No. We were here before witches were witches and words were words and the world was the world. Not Mr. Hue, of course, but the rest of us. We have been called the Wild Things, the Wrong Ones, the Widdershins, the Damps. We were the afterbirth; after Chaos came Order. We are the facilitators of that utter perfection."

"Chaos," Ennica repeated. "You're talking 'beginning of the universe' type stuff."

"A never-ending series of storms in a never-ending line of teacups. Life is Chaos. So it follows that we are Death." The witch pet the crow reverently. "He was once a majestic bird with rainbow plumage, Mr. Hue was. His first taste of carrion flesh turned him black. He is much more elegant now, don't you think?" She nuzzled his sharp beak with her nose. "Even more majestic."

The chocolate in her mouth turned to dirt, and Ennica forced herself to swallow. She had already welcomed insanity, or she would have never climbed this mountain in the first place. "Are you evil?"

"We are evil to good as night is to day and the end is to the beginning. We are solace and silence and solitude. We drew blueprints in the stars and fashioned this world from the dust, and we return all that thrives here to it. We complete the circle."

"By killing people."

"By bringing order to chaos."

"So...by killing people."

The witch shrugged. "As you wish."

"What do you get out of it? Power? Joy? Vengeance?"

"Balance," said the witch. "It is the way of things. Up, down. Life, death. Action, reaction. The reason we do what we do is because the universe could not exist without us."

"If you hate life so much, you must find me revolting."

"Not in such harsh words."

"Tell me then," said Ennica. "What do you see when you look at me?"

The witch studied her with strange eyes, bright in contrast to the dark shadows in the skin that surrounded them, but still flat, like the crow's, like the deer heads mounted in Ennica's father's garage. They burned like a fire with no flame. Like the coal, deep in the heart of the mountain beneath them.

Ennica imagined herself through those dead eyes. A short, pudgy girl with stringy hair and blotchy skin. A good heart and a soft life. A mouse in a field waiting for an eagle to prey on it, waiting to be wanted somehow, by someone. Desperate and sad and stupid and too full of dreams and fairy tales to be of much use to anyone.

"I see a mess waiting to be tidied up," said the witch. "I see a life within a life, and I pity you both."

If the witch could read her mind, then her knowledge of the pregnancy was no surprise. *Smile, baby. You've just met your first witch.* "If you find humans so unpalatable, why look like one?"

The witch folded her arms and crossed her legs under the table. Her feet were bare beneath her ragged skirts, but there wasn't a speck of dirt on them. "You came all this way to ask my story?"

"Look," said Ennica. "It's been a long day, I imagine it will be a longer night, and I have little left to lose. My mind's full of its own misery, and to be honest I'm tired of it. I would love nothing more than—okay, than my ex's head on a platter, but second to that, I'd love to hear about some troubles that aren't my own, you know?"

"I like you," said the witch with her dead eyes.

"I might like you too, but the jury's still out," said Ennica. "So spill. Why live the life of a human?"

"It is my curse," she said. The crow murmured a consoling caw.

Ennica picked up her teacup again. "Oh, this is going to be good."

"We were young," said the witch, "mere millennia old, a blink of an eye in the yawn of the universe. We were reckless, learning our boundaries, testing their resistance."

"Not so very different from humans," said Ennica.

"Only we lived deep down under the earth, in the soul of the world, in the heart of the mountain. Our paths were never meant to cross with the humans. And so it remained, until the humans discovered an aspect of our existence they couldn't live without."

"Coal."

"In our wake, we cannot help but arrange the basic elements into their purest form. Given enough time—"

"—the earth would be a diamond." Ennica's grandfather had been a miner. He'd taught her about coal, and its varying degrees of carbon purity. The purest carbon, given time and the pressure of the world above it, was a diamond.

"Unfortunately, humans evolved before that time had come to pass. They dug tunnels into our sanctuary and brought light and noise and chaos where there had once been silence."

In a twisted way, Ennica could relate. "It's never fun to have your once peaceful existence smashed to pieces by some uncaring lout."

"Exactly so. My siblings and I try and maintain our privacy when we can, in our way."

"Siblings?"

"The imp, the angel, the twins, and I."

"You lost me," said Ennica.

"You can always tell the imp's passage from his distinct odor. The angel has put so many birds to rest that she takes wing herself now, most days. The twins, they fight. Always fighting. They are the argument, and the cold shoulder."

"And you are the blackdamp," said Ennica. Her grandfather had told her stories of men killed by the damps in the mine. The stink damp reeked of sulfur. The whitedamp killed the canary before it killed you. The firedamp exploded. And the afterdamp got you when the dust settled, just when you thought you were safe. Then there was the mixture of everything, the queen of them all: the blackdamp.

The witch had called them the Wild Ones, the Widdershins, and *the Damps*. Ennica wondered what the miners would say if they knew it was vengeful fairies smothering their brothers to death in the bowels of the coal mine.

"I was always drawn to the humans; they were complicated beings, and so am I. They disgusted and repulsed me, but I was fascinated. I knew I should stay away, but I could not. " The witch cocked her head to one side, a gesture that would have looked more natural performed by Mr. Hue. "Does this make sense to you?"

Let's see: desperately wanting something you know you shouldn't, and then later being burned by same. Oh, yeah. She'd written that scene in her diary a time or two. "Yes," said Ennica.

"We are completely different," said the witch. "There is nothing of us in you, and never should be."

"Should?" asked Ennica.

"There is one thing." The witch raised a finger. "The spark. I would never have known it had I not seen it with my own eyes, for it was something I never would have guessed on my own. The Damps, we are one or we are

14

many. We are legion or solitude, at will. We are here, there, and everywhere, or nowhere, as we wish." She looked pointedly at Ennica's stomach and Ennica raised a hand, as if to shield her unborn child from those dead eyes. "We do not procreate as you do. We simply exist."

"But you know about human procreation?"

"Yes. A man and woman once came into the mine, back when the tunnels were first being shored up. There have been many since, but this one...this one was my folly. They shed their clothes and came together and created a life."

Or ruined one, thought Ennica.

The witch's eyes glowed, and suddenly did not seem as flat and lifeless as they had before. Ennica wasn't sure it was a good thing.

"The spark," said Ennica.

"I witnessed it, that one perfect moment in the midst of all that chaos when two souls came together and merged perfectly into one. And it was..."

"...a miracle," said Ennica.

"But only for that moment," said the witch. "That one, blessed moment when your species and mine suddenly have the same goal: simplicity and beauty in one perfect unity. Not long after, that unity divided into two, and then four, and again and again, creating that thing"—she looked down at herself in her gray rags—"*this* thing you call a body." She touched her arms, the skin at her throat, her face. "How can you stand to be trapped in this prison, ever slowly succumbing to entropy?"

"How did you manage to become trapped in it?"

"I was caught up in the moment. Mesmerized. When the spark was created, my essence was trapped within it, and I became its soul."

"You became that baby?"

"I became a spirit trapped in a messy carcass." She spat out the rancid words. "I did not become human."

Ennica did not want to upset the witch before she asked her request, so she kept her talking. "What happened to the soul of the baby that would have been?"

The witch blew across her fingertip as if blowing out a tiny candle flame. Though she was no longer cold, Ennica shivered.

"I was invincible. I was immortal. I was before time and after. I was perfect. And but for that one, beautiful, damning spark, I would be perfect still."

"So, if you're no longer human and no longer a Damp, what are you now?"

Dead or not, Ennica recognized the look in those eyes: that same look she had seen in the bathroom mirror, splattered with the vomit that had ricocheted off the sink after she'd found out that...after she'd found out. It was a look of confusion, devastation, and loss. And as soon as Ennica saw it, it was gone. That blissful innocence had been replaced by something stronger. Something deadlier. Something...else. Something with the power to grant wishes, to tame crows, to climb mountains.

"I don't know," said the witch. "We were not meant to feel. We were not meant to love or hate. We were simply meant to be, until the end of the universe and beyond."

"You loved?" It was impertinent to ask, but Ennica could not help herself. In a way, she was jealous. She wished she didn't have to feel anything. How much easier her life would be right now if she couldn't experience the pain of love and hate, humiliation, and responsibility.

Mr. Hue cawed again and preened himself. Had the crow been her lover? "No," said the witch. "Mr. Hue and I connect beyond trivial emotions. But I did love a man once, a human man. I yearned to hold him in my arms, to sink my hands into his flesh and watch him crumble to ash, to free him from the prison of life."

Ennica wasn't sure if she should be more worried that the witch spoke so casually of murdering her lover, or that Ennica herself wasn't moved by it. "You didn't kill him?" she asked.

"Worse," answered the witch. "I doomed him to live. I fled into these woods, as close as I could ever be again to the heart of my home, my mountain, and here I have remained."

"I'm sorry." Ennica reached her hand across the table to pat the witch's arm, give her some comfort in knowing that, for this little while at least, she was not alone. The witch's skin was cool and smooth, like marble. Like death.

Ennica bit back a sigh. Only she would be stupid enough to comfort Death.

"It is late for you," said the being to whom time meant next to nothing. "You should rest; regain your strength." She opened the door behind her, a door that had not been there until she reached for it.

The house was like the teacup of water then; it was whatever she wanted it to be. Nice. In the room was a bed, as simple a furnishing as the table at which they sat, but it would suffice. Beggars can't be choosers. Still far and away better than slowly dying outside on the frozen ground.

The teacup was now gone, as was the table. And when Ennica stood to follow the witch into the room, the chair beneath her disappeared as well. Would that certain memories could vanish just as easily.

"I will grant your wish," the witch told her. Mr. Hue cawed his concurrence from her shoulder.

Ennica had never voiced her desire aloud, but she apparently hadn't needed to. "Thank you."

"For once, I believe it is I who should be thanking you," said the witch. "Sleep well."

Ennica did sleep well; her exhaustion caught up with her the moment her head hit the thin feather pillow. But her dreams were not sweet.

As before, the shadows on the backs of her eyelids resolved themselves into Anthony and Tanya. Ennica clenched her fists as she watched them conspiring, laughing, carefree without so much as a passing worry about the innocent life—lives!—they had ruined in their selfish wake.

She was not a fairy; she was no firedamp. She could not stand aside with a soul of vapor and a heart of coal and watch, indifferently, as she doomed her lover to live out his life. She walked up to the couple, her long black skirts swirling about her legs and brushing the tops of her bare feet. With one pale arm she pushed Tanya to the side, and with the other she swept Anthony up in her cold embrace and kissed him. Through that kiss she fed him all her love and all her pain and everything else she had in her that he never did—and never would—understand.

He tasted like chocolate.

She felt his heart stop, felt his body grow cold in her arms. She felt him crumble to dust beneath her lips until there was nothing in her hands but ash. She felt the rainbow colors of the baby inside her melt away into a majestic, elegant blackness. There was no noise, no mess, and the feel of the soft soot between her fingers was ecstasy. She knelt, thrust her hand in the pile of Anthony at her feet, and pulled out the one thing that would not have turned to ash: his spark. It was a diamond now, burning with a deep, pure fire, and Ennica marveled at its perfection.

The horse woke her, nuzzling her face and shoulder and nudging her into the sunshine. The house was gone; the witch was gone. She and the horse were alone at the base of the mountain. She squinted up at the sky, up the mountain path she'd have sworn she'd climbed the day before, and then she remembered how stupid she was, and how insane, and possibly how hormonal. She shrugged it off. A shame, really, that her little adventure had all been a dream.

She slowly picked her aching body up, moaning and cursing the unforgivable ground that had been her bed and wondering where the rocks had been that made her hurt so badly. She bent and stretched, trying to work enough kinks out to remount the horse; she should really get it back to the stables before her father started to worry. As for the rest of her life...she put a hand on her belly.

Odd; she felt none of her previous hatred toward Anthony anymore. She could honestly say she no longer loved him. In fact, she didn't feel anything. She closed her eyes...and thought of an abandoned watchtower, and teacups filled with chocolate, and a stove that smelled like apple pie. All those horrible memories and terrible feelings and atrocious, nonsense fantasies were gone.

"Thank you," Ennica whispered to no one, for if it had all been a dream, there was really no one to thank. As if in reply, a crow swooped down in a whirlwind of ebony feathers and dropped a shiny object in the dirt at her feet. Cawing triumphantly, it flew away, back up the mountain, into the mists from whence it came. Ennica bent down gingerly to retrieve the diamond, and the knowledge that came with it.

She would return the horse and say her goodbyes. She would not stay for the funeral or the gossip; that was some other girl's life now. That blissful innocence had been replaced by something stronger. Something deadlier. Something...else. Something with the power to grant wishes, to tame crows, to climb mountains.

She lifted her face back up to the path through the trees and the red-tinged dawn of the new day. Somewhere on that mountain, there was a cabin waiting for her. ♟

BLACK HEART

By P.J. Hoover

"YOU KNOW IT'S GETTING LATE," Ethan says.

I ignore him because yes, I know it's getting late. I don't need him telling me for the fifteenth time. I pretend I can't hear him over the hum of the motor and look through the trees that surround me. Fog hovers over the brushy ground, like an early-morning dew that hasn't yet lifted.

"Mikayla's expecting me in a half hour," he says a little louder this time.

I cut the engine on my ATV and jump off, grabbing my phone. I am so close. In front of me stretches the longest bridge I've ever seen up here in the woods. And probably the oldest and most decrepit. The rusty iron looks like it will snap if someone steps foot on it, not to mention what the crushing weight of an ATV would do. There are patches that might at one point have been covered in concrete but are now gaping holes. I raise my phone and snap a few pictures, letting the black fog creep into the frame for effect. But the angle is off. I grab hold of the railing and give it a little push, testing it. It shakes, but just a little.

"I can cross," I say.

Behind me, Ethan jumps off his ATV and joins me. "You can give up, Autumn. The graves aren't here. They're an urban legend—nothing more."

"Most legends are based on reality," I say. I'm not sure this is entirely true, but in this case, I'm going with it. I pull up Maps on my phone and check the coordinates. They have to be right. They came from Grandpa's old maps I'd found in the attic. This is how I know it's not legend. Grandpa had come here once when he was a boy. He'd seen the graves himself. According to him, when the bodies had been found, they'd buried them on the spot and erected two stone obelisks, each nearly as tall as he was. We should be able to see them by now—at least their tops peeking through the brush—but all we've found are ancient trees, animal droppings, and ant hills the size of tractors. They have to be just on the other side of the bridge.

Ethan tries to grab my phone, but I shove it back in my pocket.

"There's no graves, Autumn," he says. "Or if there are, you're never going to find them."

He's wrong. I even checked old marriage records at the library. Back in 1890, Edward Phillips had married Annie Williams. Black Annie they'd called her since it was her fourth marriage, her other three husbands having died. According to legend, their marriage had lasted five years. Then . . . well, that's why I'm here looking for their graves.

"So, you're just giving up?"

"I'm not giving up," Ethan says. "But it's Friday night and it's getting dark and Mikayla's gonna be pissed if I'm late."

"Mikayla's psycho," I say. Which maybe isn't the nicest thing, but his girlfriend gives me dagger eyes every time I pass her in the halls. Can I help it if I'm best friends with her latest boyfriend?

Ethan grabs his water bottle and pulls the cap off. "I wish you would just try to get along with her."

I snag his open water bottle and take a long drink. "And I wish you had better taste."

Ethan laughs because it's not like he can claim Mikayla's a prize or anything. She's dated five other guys in the last four months, all of which ended in screaming fights worthy of viral videos. As far as I'm concerned, Ethan is just next in her line of samples at the Golden Chicken all-you-can-eat buffet that she views our high school as.

"There's still an hour until sunset," I say. "Let's just cross the bridge." And I give him my wide-eyed look that always makes him cave in.

He takes his water bottle back and finishes it off. "Can't."

Stupid Mikayla.

"Fine. Go," I say.

Ethan looks at me like my brain's cracked. "There is no way in hell I'm leaving you to cross the bridge alone."

I cross my arms and lean against my ATV. "I'm not giving up yet." Even though I know I should. The hunting club that leases this land has 'No Trespassing' signs posted every two feet. You'd have to be blind and illiterate to miss them.

He narrows his eyes. "You do know you're the most pig-headed person in the entire world, don't you?"

"I take that as a compliment."

"Come on, Autumn," Ethan says. He gives me my same wide-eyed look right back. "Please?"

I scowl.

"We'll come back," he says. "We can bring my dad's metal detector."

Oh, he gets me with the metal detector. If we do come back with the metal detector, we're sure to find something. Maybe even the murder weapon. If legend can be believed—which yes, it can—then the ax Annie Phillips used to off her husband was never found. Finding the head of the ax? Now that would be epic.

"When?"

He grins and thinks about it. "Next Wednesday after school?"

"I work Wednesday."

"Then Thursday."

I narrow my eyes at him. "You promise."

"I promise."

"Fine," I say. "But you can't break your promise, even if Mikayla summons you."

"I won't break it," Ethan says. "Anyway, Mikayla doesn't own me."

I'm about to ask him if he's sure about that, but I bite my tongue.

"You suck," I say instead. "I can't believe you really like her."

"Love her," he says. "I love Mikayla."

He's so sincere when he says it, but I can't help but burst out laughing. "You've been dating a month and a half, and you love her?"

Ethan crosses his arms. "Some love is meant to be." It sounds a lot like he's trying to quote Shakespeare or some bullshit like that.

I snort. "Yeah, that's what Annie Phillips said right before she chopped her husband up into little pieces. You think their love was meant to be?"

Ethan rolls his eyes. "Urban legend, remember? I think their love wasn't real."

At his words, the fog descends, and the wind rustles the leaves around us. I wrap my arms around my waist and glance around. There's someone out there. I feel them watching us.

"Ethan?" I say. I look back, toward the bridge. From the other side, a thin trail of black smoke curls toward us. It mixes with the fog, yet it's separate, moving like it has a mind of its own. And with it, carried on the wind, is the sound of a low hum, almost like the din of voices before a concert starts.

"Do you hear that?" I lower my voice.

"Hear what?" Ethan says, way too loud.

"Shhh..." I say, putting a finger to my lips and focusing. Slowly the words take shape. The voices whisper of betrayal. Of sacrifice. Of death and anger. Of revenge. The trail of smoke twists and curls, arcing around, keeping time with the voices.

"You hear it, right?" I ask.

Ethan shakes his head. "I don't hear anything."

As I watch, the trail of smoke crosses the bridge, swirls around both me and Ethan, and then streaks away. And with its departure, the voices are gone.

Goosebumps cover my arms. Maybe this is why Grandpa only came here once. Maybe he felt the same thing. I whip around the face Ethan. "You didn't see any of that?"

"Any of what, Autumn?"

I motion at the bridge, the fog, the hint of anger than hangs in the air.

"It felt like . . ."

Ethan grabs my hand, centering me. "We need to go, Autumn."

I shake my head. "It felt like hatred. Pure hatred."

He tugs on my hand. "You're letting the urban legend get to you. Now come on."

He's right. It had to be my imagination.

The fog is thick around the tires when we get back on our ATVs. We head out of the woods, leaving the bridge and any thoughts of ax murder far behind.

We're pretty far off the beaten path, so it's bumpy going with narrow ATV trails to navigate. I take the hills when I can, trying to catch a little air, grinning at Ethan when I see him doing the same. We ride without talking and cut up the back way until we finally get on the paved road to Penn Five. Ethan slows to a stop because this is where we always part ways, him on the road into town, and me off to the outskirts.

"Have fun on your date," I yell over to him.

"Call me," I think he says, because he puts his hand to his head in a phone motion.

I roll my eyes but give him a smile. And then he revs his engine and takes off, leaving me there in the Pennsylvania valley watching the sun begin to sink behind the tree line. The air's cool, so I lean back and rest on the seat, and I let the sun warm my arms. The evenings are just now shifting to cool. I swear this summer was the hottest we've had in a decade, almost like the heat was seeping up from hell. Only in the last week have I been able to open the windows at night.

I close my eyes and breathe in the cool air, trying to put the woods out of my mind. But a door slams, and I jump. My eyes snap open. I glance around, but the road is empty. Most of the houses around here are vacant, used as vacation homes. A couple weeks ago for Labor Day, it had been like one big cook out, but now they're all sealed up again. Most people won't come back from the city again until hunting season starts.

But I'm sure I heard something. My heart quickens as I hear a shuffle like a chair being dragged across a wooden porch. I rev my engine just a smidge to let whoever's out there know I'm here. I don't want to surprise someone and get shot; guns are like bling around here. But above the sound of my ATV, I don't hear anything else.

The wind picks up and sends a chill across my arms. Anger. Revenge. Hatred so thick it hangs in the air. My imagination is getting away from me.

The sun's setting, but even in the valley, it's not yet dark. The fog creeps from the woods onto the road, like a shadow drifting across the world. It must mean rain is coming, which means I should get home. I lean forward and shift into gear.

I'm five feet down the road when something moves in my peripheral vision.

"Holy shit!" I say, and my heart starts pounding in my neck.

There's a creepy old woman standing at the top of her porch, staring right at me. Old Mrs. Poliski. I'd forgotten she and her husband still live here. Most of the old families died off and left their houses to their kids by now. But not the Poliskis. If small town rumors can be believed, they're still alive, and all four of their kids are dead.

Mrs. Poliski stares at me from the porch. She's wearing beige old lady pants and a blue shirt and has an apron tied around her waist that looks like it's covered in whatever she's been cooking. She's probably just enjoyed the cool weather, like me. I'm sure their house doesn't have air conditioning, and if she's been cooking, it's got to be hot in there.

"Hi," I call even though the way she's looking at me with her glassy eyes is totally creeping me out. She's got to be about a hundred by now. My heart has slowed back to only a slightly panicked state.

Mrs. Poliski takes a step down. Toward me. But she doesn't say anything. And I can't help but notice she's holding a frying pan. It's clenched in her right hand fiercely, like it's grounding her to Earth.

I rev my engine again and decide it's time to get going.

She takes another step.

"Are you okay?" I ask. Maybe she's got Alzheimer's and needs help. I ignore the pounding inside my chest and try to be a good citizen.

Mrs. Poliski stares at her empty left hand, like she's holding a cue card, telling her what to say. Behind her, black smoke swirls in a low cloud.

"He's not moving. I don't know what happened."

My eyes flicker to the frying pan. It's got to be as old as she is and must be cast iron. But she's holding it like an extension of her arm. A wisp of black smoke escapes from it, like she's just taken it off the stove and walked out here. Which can't be right. She doesn't even have a hot pad.

"Who's not moving?" I ask. I try to infuse my thin voice with confidence, but my brain's screaming at me that something's off here.

She steps down and then plants one foot next to the other. "Frank. He won't get up."

If he's as old as she is, he could have had a heart attack. He could seriously need help. I cut the engine and jump off my ATV. I'm no expert, but I did take CPR in gym class.

"What happened?" I come up to her, but it's like she won't move out of the middle of the porch steps. Her eyes are dark and cloudy. They're looking everywhere and not seeing anything at all. Maybe she's in shock.

"He won't move," she repeats.

Time is critical. I push past her and move up the steps. They're so old, the wood feels like it won't hold my weight. But I'm up and through the front door before she can turn around.

The house has three rooms on the bottom floor, but it only takes me a second to find Mr. Poliski. He's lying on the kitchen floor face-down. I rush over to him hoping I'm not too late, but I stop in my tracks. The entire back of his head is bashed in. His hair is a mass of sticky red with bits of brains mixed in. Blood is splattered everywhere. One of his eyeballs lays about a foot away from his head.

This was no heart attack.

This was . . .

"He won't get up."

I turn at the sound of her voice. Mrs. Poliski stands there with her frying pan looking down at him. Her black smoky eyes are fixed on the body on the floor. My breathing almost stops as my eyes drift once again to the pan. It looks like the bottom is covered in food.

"Stay away from me." I take a step backward, but the kitchen's so small there's only me and Mr. Poliski and a blood-spattered wood-burning stove filling up the space.

"He wouldn't listen," she says.

"Go back outside," I manage to say. I can't get outside unless she gets out of the doorframe. The heat from the stove makes my head spin.

"I loved him," she says. "But she made me do it."

Bile rises into my throat, and I'm sure I'm going to throw up. Red fills my vision until it's just a tunnel that I need to get through to get out of here. But there's only one door, and she's in the way.

"You did this. You killed him," I say. I reach to my pocket for my phone, but it's not there. I take another step backwards, but my foot slips out from under me and I'm on the floor right next to her dead husband. My hands catch my fall, but the floor is covered in his blood. Each breath I take is like a gasp, and I think she's going to kill me next. I glance at him, wondering if there's any chance he's still alive, but nothing moves. I scoot sideways away from him. Mrs. Poliski moves forward. She lifts her frying pan so I can see the entire cast iron bottom of it. It's not covered in food. It's sticky red blood. Blood and everything else that was inside Mr. Poliski's head.

"I loved him," she says. "A long time ago. She told me this was how we could be together forever."

Holy shit, this woman has just murdered her husband.

I grab the stove but pull my hands back; it's burning hot. I push off the floor, and I'm to my feet and moving toward the door. Either I'll get out of here alive or Mrs. Poliski will smash my head in, too. I shove past her and am out the screen door and down the steps so fast I jump them. Images of brains covering the floor fill my mind, and I throw up in the front yard. Gobs and chunks just like Mr. Poliski's brains. I wipe my mouth and try to focus as I stumble to my ATV.

My phone's sitting there on the seat of my ATV. I grab it and dial 911.

"911. What is your emergency?"

Each word is like hiking up a mountain, but I get them out. Tell them my location. Try to describe what happened. Then I hang up. I try not to look back at the house. But the wind picks up, and carried on it are voices. They're more frantic now, whispering of anger, revenge. Love gone wrong.

I turn slowly. Mrs. Poliski stands there on her front porch, now clutching a butcher knife. Behind her, drifting through the screen door is a thin trail of black smoke. The same smoke I'd seen up in the woods. It filters out the door, twists around Mrs. Poliski in a large arc. As it does, her eyes clear and she smiles. Contentment fills her face, and she lets out a deep sigh.

"Together forever," she says. Then she draws the knife across her throat.

I scream as Mrs. Poliski falls to the ground. Then the black smoke swirls around her one final time and darts off, heading back toward the woods whence it came. ♜

BLACK SAILS

By Teel James Glenn

"THERE ARE SEVERAL WHITE SAILS approaching, Medea," the Artificial Liaison Program said.

"You know you don't have to tell me about every little piece of space debris, Alp," Medea Addison said as she removed her workout clothes and dropped them in the hamper. She plugged her next lesson chem-tube into her data feed port so she could absorb the lesson while she was worked on and then climbed up onto the medical table.

"I realize that, miss," Alp said, "but I also know you like to be kept informed; after all I wish to do my best to take care of you."

She laughed, "Yes *you* do, Alp, and a good job you do of it. So today, I need a deep massage; it was a hard workout."

"I remember," Alp said as it extended the massage tentacles from the top of the table to work their way along the sore muscles of the station attendant's back. "You fought the interface droid with great skill."

The dark-haired Medea stretched on the bed as the flexible manipulators of Alp worked her back while playing a soft jazz score it improvised from pre-recorded notes it had reassembled into a new tune.

As the station attendant, Medea had to monitor the mining systems and the communication relays at the recharging station. It was a position mandated by law to have a human on site, but it was a lonely life for the station monitor with only the usual monthly mining trawlers and the supply ships and occasional other craft in the sector.

Alp, having been grown from a map of her neural network to sync him to her mind, worked hard to anticipate her needs and wants. She was also working toward an astrophysics degree between her duties so she would be set when she got home, absorbing the information with chemical drips and with pre-recorded 3D modules for practical tests.

She was halfway through her four-year tour, but it was not as bad as it might have been with the pay accumulating for her planet side landfall, and best of all, there was someone special who stopped by every couple of weeks to brighten her life. Thaddeus! Though it was for only a few nights at a time while he was on his own rounds with his freighter, they'd had immediate chemistry when he stopped by on the first supply run of her posting.

"Do the muscles feel better?" Alp asked.

In fact, Alp already knew how she felt, for the program had sensors that allowed it to monitor skin temperature, blood flow and endorphin levels so the program could 'sense' her moods and feelings with considerable accuracy. He did, after all, think exactly as she did, for, as they used to say, they were of 'one mind.'

"Oh yes," she sighed. "You take good care of me, Alp."

"I am glad," Alp said. "It is my purpose."

The jazz music was a soothing blanket of sound and the woman enjoyed it until Alp's voice- though always without inflection or intensity—broke in with words that seemed to convey a sense of urgency.

"Black Sails approaching, Medea."

"You sure?"

"Large enough debris to require authorization, my dear."

"Okay," she said, reluctantly rising from the med-bed. "The law is the law. Set up the screen, and I'll check them."

The woman padded barefoot down the hall from the medical bay to the control room where the sectors of sky above the remote station were indicated on the radar screens. The images were mere colored blips but even as she entered the room Medea could see that they were barely over the size of incoming flotsam that fell into the realm of 'manual destruction'- that is, over the two-meter size that might indicate a life pod.

Medea looked at the silhouettes of the 'black sails' – the images that might be ships- and nodded to the ever-present Alp. "Okay, those are just space junk of some sort. Consider them black sails, Alp, zap'em."

"Consider them 'zapped', Medea." The program said. A moment later the orbiting defense satellites went into operation and the two blips were gone.

"I'm gonna shower and then I'd like a meal, Alp," she said. "Veal, I think. And then I'm gonna do my hair—I think the Argo is due tomorrow."

"It is indeed on the schedule for Mr. Thaddeus to arrive in The Argo in this rotation."

"Yes, he is," she giggled and did a little happy dance. "Rotation indeed!"

Alp noted the blood pressure spike and sudden release of endorphins at the prospect of seeing the engineer of the cargo ship.

The program prepared the meal and Medea showered and did her hair to a more upbeat jazz score. While she ate, she spoke to Alp about the schedule of ships coming through the charging station over the next two weeks.

"Our busy season," she said. "Hmm—you are getting better with the Veal Marsala," she said. "You'll have to make it when Thad is here."

"I have adjusted ingredients to your taste, Medea," Alp said. "I will make sure I have this ready for you and your guest."

"Thanks, Alp."

When she had finished eating the station worker watched a holo-cube story and then drifted off to sleep to the strains of soft classical music.

Medea woke early with the excitement of a child on Christmas morning and quickly went through her waking routine at the com station, checking all the 'overnight' reports from Alp.

"All was routine, Medea," Alp said when she finished.

"And?"

"And The Argo is two hours out from orbital position."

"Wahoo!" She jumped up from the console. "I'm gonna make myself presentable," she said as she headed out of the room.

"You are always presentable," Alp said.

"Too kind, sir," she said as she all but skipped to her berth to do her hair and actually apply make up, something she only did when Thad visited.

Alp cycled through the regular station preparations to beam up power to the arriving ship and prepared a list of supplies for the shuttle to bring down, talking to The Argo's automated systems.

Then the call came over the video screen. "Argo One on approach." The bearded face of Thaddeus Arnold beamed a wide smile. Medea did not turn on her upfeed but opened audio only.

"Hey there, stranger," she said. "How far out?"

"Argo in high orbit," he said, "and Argo One is entering the exosphere with ETA of twenty standard minutes. Over."

"And in my arms in twenty-one, over!"

"And out!"

Medea had a hard time concentrating on the dock port acceptance protocols while she waited for twenty long minutes, but Alp corrected her minor control mistakes.

"He is almost here, Alp," she said.

"Yes, Medea," Alp said. "I can handle the automated acceptance from here on out; you may head to the bay."

"Thanks, Alp!" She raced from the control room down the corridor and waited at the airlock to the landing bay while the shuttle from the cargo ship settled into the docking bay.

Alp noted her spike in blood pressure and skin temperature the moment the door to the bay opened and Medea all but leapt into the arms of Thaddeus.

It spiked even more as his powerful arms enveloped her and pulled her up off the deck for an impassioned kiss.

"I've missed you," she managed to say when she came up for air. "So much!"

He made no reply, but simply picked her up into his arms and carried her down the corridor to her sleeping quarters. Once there the two had no energy for words as they stripped and all but devoured each other in passionate embraces.

While the two sated their physical appetites Alp continued processing the automated charging requests from The Argo, beaming up energy to the ship, off-loading the physical supplies from the shuttlecraft and monitoring the mining operations.

Afterward, when the two humans rested beside each other Alp piped relaxing music into the sleeping room.

"I swear," Medea said as she lay her head on Thad's chest, "I think I would go mad if I could not look forward to your visits."

"You were fine before I came along," he said quietly.

"I suppose," she said, then giggled, "But I didn't know what I was missing."

He sat up and washed in the shower while they talked. "I am afraid this is a really short stay," he said. "They tightened the schedule on this run to get my cargo back by eclipse at home."

"What do you mean, short stay?" She stepped in the shower with him and set to scrubbing his back unbidden.

"I pretty much have to head right back up," he said.

"No!"

"Yes, sorry. Actually, I really should not have stopped by at all and called in the order and sent a drone instead; I really didn't need the top off of the fuel cells on The Argo."

"No!" she stepped out of the shower and dried her hair as he quickly toweled himself dry and then started putting his uniform back on. "Yes."

"Well, when will you be back this way?"

He started for the door of the room and stopped in the entranceway. He seemed to struggle for words and then finally said, "I won't be coming back this way, Medea."

"What?"

"I-uh—I'm going planet side to be married."

"What!" She quickly wrapped a towel around herself, and then raced towards Thad to take hold of his jacket sleeve.

"What do you mean you're getting married?"

He pulled away from her grasp. "Yes, just what I said, I'm getting married."

"But-you never—"

"I didn't think it mattered, Medea," he said with a shrug as he walked down the corridor toward the launch bay.

"All supplies are off-loaded," Alp announced. "The Argo One is fully recharged for flight."

"Didn't matter?" Medea screamed. She followed him still only wrapped in the towel to the airlock door. "How does what we have not matter?"

"It was fun but-"

"Fun!" She charged him and tried to pummel him with her fists, but he avoided her attack and pushed her back so that she collapsed against the bulkhead sobbing. "You son of a—"

"Get control of yourself," he said in a cold voice. "I never promised you anything more than the time we had together. It was just sex."

"Never?" She sobbed, "How could you think it was just sex?"

He had opened the airlock now and stepped through to the bay. "I came down just to tell you in person and I...I was just going to tell you first thing but—"

He held the closing door from sliding closed until he said, "—but it was a nice way to say goodbye." Then the portal was closed, and she stood stunned and alone as he cycled through the lock and headed out to his ship.

Alp monitored the state of her blood pressure and noted the endorphin level drop in the woman.

"Damn you!" she muttered, as she entered her sleeping quarters, "I hate you, I hate you! I wish I was dead. I wish you were dead!"

She threw herself down onto her bed and started to cry, her body wracked with sobs.

"I am sorry for your discomfort, Medea," Alp said. "If there is anything I can do to help you, I will do it." Without being told, Alp flooded the room with positive ions, jazz music and dimmed the lights.

"No!" she cried. "He lied to me! He used me." She kept crying, but with lessening intensity.

In the control room the screens showed The Argo One dock with the main ship and begin to move out of orbit.

Suddenly a recording of Medea's voice filled the room. "Consider them black sails, Alp, zep 'em." The orbital debris system was activated. Streams of protons fired, and The Argo disappeared from the screen.

Alp released some mild sedative into the air filtration system and Medea was soon sleeping peacefully.

"I wish to do my best to take care of you, Medea," Alp said. "It is my purpose." ♜

SEVEN ENTRIES IN
THE MIDNIGHT PATH

By Jeremiah Dylan Cook

**EVIDENCE IDENTIFICATION NUMBER 03051970 – 09/13/2019 –
12:00 P.M.** – The journal below was written by Ms. Jennifer Tillinghast.
Ms. Tillinghast vanished amidst an outbreak of violence at the Board Game
Coffee House on 03/13/2015. Ms. Tillinghast was previously sought for
questioning in relation to the murder of Lisa Barron, the lover of her ex-
husband, Kevin Upton. Ms. Tillinghast's journal was found in a gas station
near Bird City, Kansas, and forwarded to the Hazel Peak Police Department
by Kansas Highway Patrol. Ms. Tillinghast's former psychologist, Dr. Kiste,
has made notes between the journal entries to provide greater insight into
Ms. Tillinghast's thinking.

Entry 1 – Saturday, March 7th

My therapist suggested I start journaling. Her instructions were to
record a day and then flip the page and forget about it. I'm only supposed
to review my scribblings at the end of the week. Hopefully, I'll see some
healing progress in the tapestry of journal entries. It's all supposed to help
me move past the incident, although she objects to my name for that day.
She says I'm empowering the event, but I can't seem to find a better word

for "the day you got a text message meant for your husband's fuckbuddy." *Incident* works fine for me.

Whatever you want to call that day, I've been solo since. Readjusting to living alone has been strange after five years of cohabitation. At first, I was almost happy. There wasn't anyone leaving dirty dishes in the sink, losing things around the house, or distracting me from reading, but I've been lonely the last few days.

The highlight of my first day journaling was finding an old book called *The Midnight Path* down at Cupboard Books. I've always been fascinated by occultists like Aleister Crowley, and this book is the autobiography of one of his peers. The man's name was Jean Tremblay. He was born in France, but he ended up moving across the English Channel before finding his way into Crowley's circle for a time. Eventually, he ended up residing in New York City. There, Jean grew in magical reputation until famous residents were visiting him. The entirety of Tammany Hall was rumored to attend his monthly parties at the Chelsea Hotel. During the height of his notoriety in 1925, he vanished.

The Midnight Path was found six decades later in a gas station near Bird City, Kansas. Extensive handwriting analysis established the autobiography as authentic, and the book was quickly reprinted by an enterprising small press. Unfortunately, the Satanic Panic killed any market for the book, and the print run ended up extremely small. All of this is what I remember from the Wikipedia page, but I've always found the topic fascinating, and I was toying with creating a board game based on the subject. It might give me something to do with all my newfound free time. I'm going to try and start reading the book tonight.

Until tomorrow,

J. T.

Dr. Kiste's Notes: Jennifer's situation was not uncommon. I have dealt with many wives who have had cheating husbands. The exercise I assigned was intended to allow Jennifer to work through her feelings and provide the distance for her to reassess her emotions once the week elapsed. Past patients have responded extraordinarily well to this undertaking. Based on this first entry, I don't see any issues in Jennifer's thinking. I should note that Jennifer's journal being found in the same location as the original version of *The Midnight Path* is unlikely to have been a coincidence. I assume Jennifer left this journal there intentionally.

Entry 2 – Sunday, March 8ᵗʰ

    I can't help thinking about what my ex-husband might be doing. As much as I hate that he cheated on me for weeks, I still miss the couple's shorthand we hand. The way I could give him a look and communicate how annoyed I was with our mutual friend Carol's latest boy drama. The way he could grab my thigh in just the right spot to let me know he wanted to screw. The sex was great, and what's horrible is that I noticed how exciting it'd gotten during the time he was cheating on me. He was trying all these new moves in the bedroom, and I loved them. It was only after I found out about Lisa that I realized where they were coming from. Now thinking about our sex life makes me want to puke.

    Today's been tough. I've been dwelling way too much. I took some time off work to focus on some of my hobbies, relax, and get over Kevin, but I'm quickly realizing all this time alone is a bad idea. Maybe I'll take a trip to grab a good hoagie from that pizza shop downtown tomorrow? They make the best food. This probably isn't the kind of thing my therapist wants me writing in here, but hey, it's my journal.

    Here's something weird. I found a copy of *The Midnight Path* on my bedside table this morning. I've heard about the book before, and I've always wanted to review a copy, but I have no clue how this got here. Maybe it's a parting gift from Kevin? He does still have a key to the house. Anyway, the book was written by an occultist, and he vanished under mysterious circumstances before this autobiography appeared years later. Spooky stuff. So, naturally, I can't wait to read it. Maybe I'll dive into the pages tonight. It should make for some good bedtime reading.

    Until tomorrow,

    J.T.

SEVEN ENTRIES IN THE MIDNIGHT PATH

Dr. Kiste's Notes: It is not uncommon for spouses who have been cheated on to still want their partner back. It is a little surprising how open Jennifer is about her sex life above as she would not speak about it in our sessions. This is a significant reason why the journaling exercise is successful. It makes patients discuss their issues as if no one is listening. Of course, the most severe red flag in this entry is that Jennifer has forgotten that she bought *The Midnight Path* the day prior. This is a sign that the stresses of her divorce were more significant than I initially realized.

Entry 3 – Monday, March 9ᵗʰ

Went to the pizza shop, Two Uncles, and got an Italian hoagie today. Tasted great. They make the best subs. The bread is shipped in from somewhere special. Philadelphia maybe? Does Philadelphia have good bread? Anyway, while I was there, the owner asked how my husband was doing. I stammered through an awkward explanation the guy didn't need. I could've gotten out of there with a simple "we split up." Instead, I gave him the whole story. By the time I was done recounting everything, there was a line of people jammed behind me. Completely embarrassing. Why am I so awkward? Ironically, the one person who'd understand this is Kevin. I want to call him, but I can't help feeling like he'd win the battle of wills if I did that. He messed up, and he should be the one to come back to me. He won't, of course.

Since I got home, I've been endeavoring to forget the Two Uncles fiasco. I started working on a board game based on this occultist I always found fascinating, Jean Tremblay. Kevin introduced me to board games, but I went crazy for them, whereas he lost interest. Making my own game has been a dream of mine for a while now. I don't feel like writing Tremblay's entire backstory in my journal, but he's an interesting historical figure. The game puts players in his disciples' shoes, trying to curry his favor, learn spells, and pay off corrupt New York City politicians. If players learn too many evil spells, they start to become tainted by darkness, which means they spend the rest of the game being hunted by The Midnight God. They need to use magic points to keep the creature off their trail.

Well, that's just a rough outline of the game. I started assembling my prototype today. It's all based on real-life occultism, specifically Tremblay's beliefs. I was inspired to start working on the game when I found his autobiography, *The Midnight Path*, on my front doorstep. I must've bought a copy online recently, but I can't recall when. Things have been crazy with the divorce, so this could've slipped my mind. That said, I would love to figure out the company that shipped the book to me because it was beaten up. There are scorch marks and scratches all over it. Regardless, I'm planning to dive into this for my evening's reading.

Until tomorrow,

J.T.

Dr. Kiste's Notes: In this entry, I was happy that Jennifer gave herself a project to focus on. Unfortunately, her memory issue continues. I can only posit that Jennifer was the person responsible for damaging her copy of *The Midnight Path* during the previous night.

Entry 4 – Tuesday, March 10ᵗʰ

Three days gone, and I've avoided looking back at any of my past entries. I can't say it's been that hard so far. Anyway, I'm feeling good now. I'm not going to pretend I haven't thought about Kevin on and off, but my thoughts about him felt a little less dire today.

I continued to tinker on my board game today. The Midnight Path is developing into quite a compelling little project. I might bring it out to the Board Game Coffee House for a playtest soon. The owner is super friendly, and he's great about encouraging new game designers with tips. I never could've done as much work on a project like this if my husband was still here. He always distracted me from my passions. Now I'm free to do what I want when I want. Although, I can't blame anyone else when something's wrong in the house now.

The front door was open when I woke up today. It wasn't swinging in the wind or anything like that, but it was open a fair crack. I spent the early part of the day looking for any critters that might've gotten in overnight. No idea how I managed to leave it open like that. Reminds me of the time I left my car running all night. Unlike that instance, I don't have any drugs to thank for this mistake.

One good thing did come out of the error, though. While I was poking around the house, I found my small, locked safe under my bed. I always kept it in the closet, and I don't know how it got moved under the bed. When I opened it, I found a stack of papers I'd never seen before. At first, I was a little freaked out, but then I remembered Kevin used to have a key to the safe too. He must've moved it and hidden these in there before he killed our relationship.

As far as I can tell, the papers are from the autobiography of Jean Tremblay, the guy whose life I'm basing my board game off. Kevin must've intended to bind them and give them to me for my birthday. I know I should probably feel sad to have found a lost present from my ex-husband, but I'm just so excited to get to read this. Copies are incredibly hard to find. I remember coming across one in Cupboard Books at some point in the past. I can't remember why I didn't pick it up at the time. Well, I'm spending my night reading this.

Until tomorrow,

J.T.

Dr. Kiste's Notes: It is exceptionally odd that Jennifer remembers working on a board game based on Jean Tremblay's work, but she cannot recall buying his book. There are also suggestions that Jennifer was having some sort of intense nighttime episodes. It appears that *The Midnight Path* was seriously worsened from its condition the previous night.

Entry 5 – Wednesday, March 11th

It's raining outside today. I've only managed to make it from my bed to the couch. Kevin would always talk me off the ledge when I fell into these moods before. Now, I've got no one to call. I left all my friendships on the side of the road when things got serious with the lost love. This serves me right, I guess.

I thought about tinkering with my board game, but I found it smashed to pieces. I'm not sure what the hell happened to it. Maybe an earthquake in the night? Big gust of wind? My own shoddy craftsmanship? I don't think Kevin is so vindictive that he'd break in just to smash something that was bringing me joy. At least, I hope he isn't. Probably for the best anyway. It was a complicated game. Who was I kidding? Why did I think I had any talent or ability to make something anyone else would enjoy? I'm destined to stay working in an office as a wage slave until I drop dead.

This world tells you that you can do whatever you want, but that's bullshit. You can only go as far as your family's status and wealth will allow. Born middle class? Tough luck, you'll be working a menial job until you drop dead to pay for the college degree you needed to get the menial job. It's all one big trap, and I can't help thinking we deserve a button to stop the ride and let ourselves off.

Fuck. I miss Kevin. Why did he cheat on me? Did he tire of being with someone who wasn't a bubbly, cookie-cutter member of consumer society?

I guess the only thing of interest that I can write about today, besides the black hole in my chest swallowing my happiness, is the fact that I found a few scattered pages of a book near the couch. I think they might be excerpts from the autobiography I was basing my board game on, *The Midnight Path* by Jean Tremblay. I'm not entirely sure yet, but if I can get myself off the couch, I will try to see if there are more pages around. The only weird thing about this is that I don't remember ever owning or bringing home anything related to that book. It's ridiculously hard to find. Maybe I'll call Kevin today, just to make sure he didn't stop by and drop it off without me realizing.

Until tomorrow,

J.T.

Dr. Kiste's Notes: Here, Jennifer slips into a depression. It appears her already fragile mood is impacted by the weather. Once again, Jennifer seems to have tried to harm *The Midnight Path* between entries and forgot she owned it. It's not impossible that Jennifer wrote this journal with the intention of confusing those who read it, but my opinion is that she was suffering through nightly fugue states.

Entry 6 – Thursday, March 12th

Well, per my therapist's instruction, this is the last entry I need to record before reviewing the previous pages to look for catharsis. Tomorrow, expect me to write something profound about what this breakup has meant. While I know I've still got a long way to go, I'm feeling better today than yesterday.

I woke up on the couch around midnight and realized I'd wasted my entire day feeling miserable. Time is the one thing you really can't get back in this life. It's the one personal resource we shouldn't undervalue. So, when I woke up in the middle of the night, I brewed some coffee and went about setting things right.

First, I rebuilt my board game. I even made some excellent modifications to it. I think people will really respond to this version. Then, I quit my job. Yeah, I know it's a bold step, but I just can't go back to that place and act like a drone for the rest of my life. Game designing is my passion, and I will sink or swim in that field. Lastly, when the morning arrived, I gave Kevin a call. I know. Not a good idea.

But the conversation was amicable, and I think enough time had passed that we were able to really discuss what happened. He'd said my anger and depression at where I was in life had started to rub off on him. I apologized. Oddly, the conversation took a sexual turn near the end. He told me Lisa didn't please him, and he was really missing our time together. I was advised to make these entries entirely honest, so I'll admit that I met up with Kevin this afternoon, and we were intimate. God, it hadn't been that great since we'd first met. And I felt so empowered knowing that he was now cheating with me.

Afterward, I even showed Kevin my game. He loved it. He's never loved any of my projects before. After playing, Kevin seemed different somehow. Calmer maybe? I asked what our fling meant, and he told me he planned to end things with Lisa and return tomorrow.

I've won him back, and he won't leave me again. Not after everything we've gone through. He's even agreed to support me while I create games. It's going to be better than ever.

I spent the rest of the day cleaning up the house in preparation for his return. Thankfully, I hadn't yet thrown out any of the stuff he'd failed to take with him when he left. I restored it all to its rightful place. In the process of cleaning up the house, I collected a ton of pages from a book I think might be *The Midnight Path*, the basis of my board game. I have no idea how they ended up in my house, but I'm attempting to reassemble them. There are burn marks on some of the pages, and a few are cut up. It looks like someone went through a lot of effort to wreck and scatter these throughout my home, but I've been here for a week and haven't noticed any signs of a break-in. Why would someone risk jail just to hide ruined pages anyway?

Since Kevin and I were back on good terms, I called him about the book scraps. He told me I needed to read through the pages. Kevin said the game I'd made managed to convey the book's message to him, but I needed to fully understand it myself. I was a bit perplexed, but I loved that he suddenly shared my passion for Jean Tremblay. So, I'm stapling this book back together and diving into it tonight.

Until tomorrow,

J.T.

Dr. Kiste's Notes: This entry is exciting to start with because Jennifer seems to have come out of her depression ready to re-take control of her life. Unfortunately, reaching out to Kevin appears to have been a significant step backward on her road to recovering from the divorce. Kevin's actions are typical of a serial adulterer as he jumps at the chance to cheat on his current lover with his ex. It's odd that Jennifer didn't seem to have any negative feelings about this. Once again, Jean Tremblay's book appears as if Jennifer has no recollection of buying it. Furthermore, it seems as if she'd tried to violently exorcize the book from her life the night before. Jennifer's continued attempts to rationalize what is happening are extremely concerning. It appears she may have slipped into a severe delusion. As is popularly accepted, people with serious mental disorders don't often recognize that they have them, and this journal clearly illustrates Jennifer was unaware of her own growing instability. As to Kevin's newfound interest in Jean Tremblay, I believe he was lying to get back into the good graces of Jennifer.

Entry 7 – Friday, March 13th

What the fuck? I just reviewed my previous entries. I don't remember buying *The Midnight Path* at Cupboard Books. I don't remember ever trying to read it. Everything else in the pages is precisely what happened, but all my mentions of Jean Tremblay's book are total mysteries to me. Am I losing my mind? Was someone else breaking in and swapping my journal with a forged one? Could this have been Kevin's doing? I guess that would fit, considering what happened last night.

Kevin went back to Lisa after our time together, and he took a power drill to her left eyeball. He must've been having a breakdown for a while. His cheating could've been the first sign, and I completely missed it.

Of course, the cops seem suspicious of me. I'm sure they think we conspired to get Lisa out of the picture, but they aren't arresting me yet because Kevin made no attempt to conceal the murder. He apparently killed Lisa with the front door wide open, and the neighbors phoned the cops. Kevin didn't resist when the police arrived, but they said he looked like he was coming off a manic episode. I'd never noticed him having mood changes like that before. I was always the one whose emotions swung like an amusement park pirate ship. They think something snapped inside of him. Apparently, he kept babbling about my board game. I showed it to the cops and told them everything about our day yesterday. I even showed them my sixth journal entry. They said they'd be back soon with further questions, and they'll need to collect my journal and game as evidence. No way in hell I'm letting that happen. The game is the first thing I've ever made that anyone's liked.

So, I'm going to bring it straight to the Board Game Coffee House and get as many people as possible to playtest it. Jean Tremblay would want me to spread his message.

I'm shocked at how invigorated I feel by this decision and everything that's happened today. Lisa is dead, and Kevin will be locked up. A fitting end for a woman who took what wasn't hers and a husband who cheated.

I'm cured. The source of my pain is gone, and I have a new passion in my life. Hell, there are plenty of blank pages left here for me to start my own gospel. It will be the beginning of my own version of *The Midnight Path*.

Until tomorrow,

J.T.

Dr. Kiste's Notes: This entry is, of course, the most concerning. Initially, it appears Jennifer is facing the delusion she has created regarding her copy of *The Midnight Path*, but then she is consumed by it. Her excitement over Lisa's death shows latent sociopathic tendencies, and she appears to adopt Jean Tremblay as her personal prophet. It should be noted that this fascination with Jean Tremblay may be why she only wrote her name out as J.T. in the journal. Perhaps, she wanted to revel in the fact that she had the same initials as the object of her obsession. Of course, while this journal points to a deranged mind, it is unknown how Jennifer Tillinghast managed to convey her insanity to others. Six customers were killed by people who played her board game version of *The Midnight Path* on 03/13/2015. In addition, Jennifer and her game have yet to be located. Procuring and reading a copy of Jean Tremblay's *The Midnight Path* will allow me to gain further insight into Jennifer's mind. I have already ordered a copy to review. ♜

CHOICES

By Will McDermott

THREE WINDOWS EXPLODED ABOVE JACK Lynch. Gouts of flame shot into the air as glass, wood, and metal crashed to the street around him.

"Lynch!" yelled the chief. "Lynch! Wake up."

Smoke billowed from the windows as Jack stared at the squat, brick building. Smoke of another kind filled his brain. Smoke from the past parted like a curtain, letting the present waft past Jack as the two realities reordered themselves around him.

Acrid air coated his mouth, throat, and nostrils. Yet Jack just stared, not even blinking away the tears that welled up in the corners of his eyes.

"Lynch!" yelled the chief again. "You with us on this or not?"

As the smoke cleared in Jack's brain, he reconnected with the current situation. The chief had been yelling his name for quite some time. *Damn. It happened again*, he thought.

It would take time to remember all the changes, but time was a luxury he didn't have right now. He was needed. "What's the situation, chief?" he asked, hoping Andrews hadn't already told him.

Chief Andrews wiped a meaty, black hand across his sweaty brow before shaking his head in disgust. "It's not your first meth lab fire, Lynch," he said. "Stop gawking like a damn tourist. We got reports of people holed up on the fourth floor. Take Terelli and Hogan. Sweep that floor before the fire burns through."

Jack grabbed his helmet and turned to leave, barely hearing the chief's final order. "No heroes, Lynch. Get in. Get out. Keep your men safe."

Don't worry, he thought as a portion of his previous past loomed large in his memory. *Nobody's going to die. Not this time.* He motioned his crew over to the truck. "Frank. Bill." He called. "We've got a slam and sweep. Suit up." Jack briefed his men as they strapped on oxygen tanks and donned masks. He checked their seals and hoses and gave each man a thumbs up.

As the crew moved inside, Jack concentrated on recalling his day. He remembered the building. An abandoned factory. But nothing stayed empty long in a city of ten million. This had become a hive for off-the-book activities and off-the-radar individuals. As usual, firefighters had to deal with the derelicts of the city — both living and non-living.

But Jack wouldn't give up this life for anything or anyone. A fact his wife, Maria, knew all too well. She called him a thrill-seeker...and not in a good way. But Jack couldn't quit. Maybe this job started because he was a thrill-seeker, but it had grown into so much more. It had grown into his purpose in life, his mission. He was a lifesaver, and that meant everything to Jack. He knew in his heart that was why he'd been given the gift — so he could save lives.

Two separate sets of memories shifted around inside Jack's mind. He tried to sort it all out as they entered the wide-open, factory floor.

#   #   #

He'd had another fight with Maria that morning and left the station against protocol to boot. But he had to talk her out of going on that stupid business trip.

"What's so important about this trip?" he had asked, grabbing the suitcase from her.

She tried to pull it back but was no match for his strength. Thick, black hair whipped around her oval face as a fire burned behind her big, brown eyes. "It's an important client, Jack."

Maria gave up on the suitcase with a huff and turned to pull another from the closet. "Blaine thinks we should..."

"Blaine!" Jack threw the suitcase at the bed, missing the mattress and putting a dent in the wall instead. "It's always Blaine. Blaine wants this. Blaine wants that. This is the third trip you've taken with Blaine this month. What, are you sleeping with him? Is that how you got the promotion?"

Jack knew he shouldn't have said it. Knew it even before the second suitcase came hurtling at his head. It had just come out, like he wasn't in control of his voice anymore. Fear and anger had taken over. Fear of losing her. Anger at losing her to Blaine.

The resulting apology sounded hollow, even to him.

#   #   #

"Not that way," said Jack, returning to the present.

After sweeping the factory floor — the derelicts of old machinery looming like monsters in the smokey haze — they'd moved to the second-floor offices.

The fire had started above this floor, so other than a few strands of flame licking at the corners of the drop ceilings in the back offices, they encountered nothing dangerous here and no civilians.

Bill and Frank were just about to continue up the rear staircase when something nagged at Jack from his other past. Something bad. "It...um... looks unstable," he said. "This way."

He led the way back down the corridor toward the front stairs. Frank and Bill followed along. "Whatever you say, Jack," said Frank. "You're the psycho...I mean psychic."

Jack could feel Frank's smirk burning a hole in his helmet. Behind them, almost as a counterpoint, the stairwell collapsed with a roar. Metal scraped against stone in an eerie wail. The backwash propelled smoke and debris at the men, pelting their backs as they ran.

"Jesus, Mary, and Joseph," said Frank.

Bill agreed with a simple whistle and, "Shit."

That's one, thought Jack. He pushed on as his previous past continued to replay inside his mind.

#   #   #

The argument spilled out onto the street as Maria hauled her luggage to the curb. Jack had resorted to pleading.

"Don't go," he said. "Just this once let someone else handle it. I'm off rotation tonight. We can work this out when my shift is over. We can spend all week together...and talk."

He grabbed Maria as she raised her hand to hail a cab and twirled her around to face him. "Give us time to work things out," he begged.

Her glare told him to let go, but instead he held on, as if trying to hold his marriage together by brute force. Maria squirmed and tried to wriggle free, fuming so much her olive skin turned ruddy brown. Unable to break his grip, she slammed the heel of her Manolos onto his toes.

Jack fell to the ground and held his aching foot while his fiery wife climbed into the cab.

"I'm sorry," he said, and meant it. He'd made many mistakes in his marriage but holding Maria against her will was one step too far and Jack knew it. Tears welled up in his eyes, which he quickly wiped away with the back of his hand. He told himself it was from the pain in his foot.

As the cab pulled away, Maria looked back at him. Whether she saw the tears or had been moved by the sincerity of his apology he never knew. But the cab stopped halfway down the block, and she got out.

A ray of sunlight broke through a cloud as she helped him to his feet, limning her head like an angel — a fierce, Italian angel. She put her arm around his waist. "Come on, Irish," she said. "Let's get some ice on that foot."

Jack smiled as tears dripped from his cheek onto his uniform. He picked Maria up in a fireman carry and then grabbed her bags with his free hand.

Everything was all right with the world. At least until the sirens wailed down the street. He ran to the window and saw Frank driving old number nine past the apartment. "Damn!" Jack uttered. "Andrews will have my ass."

#   #   #

The firemen moved through the smoke-filled corridor of the third floor, checking each door for heat before slamming it open and calling to anyone who might be inside. In between the noise, they listened for yells, cries, or moans.

The back wall and stairwell were encased in sheets of flames. The heat and the creaking of the floor joists kept them from reaching the last two offices.

Jack motioned back to the clear stairs behind them. "Last floor," he said. "Let's make it quick."

As they climbed, the heat pressed in, making Jack's breath come harder. He was sweating so much his visor began to fog up. As his crew reached the landing, Jack looked around to get his bearings. Six doors on each side of the hallway. At the far end, a gaping hole where the rear staircase had once been.

Molten plaster dripped from the ceiling, while dingy, green wallpaper curled and blackened as it slid toward the floor. They were directly beneath the meth lab inferno.

Bill and Frank fanned out to either side to kick open the first two doors. "Not that one!" yelled Jack. He rushed forward, diving and tackling Frank around the waist as he raised his foot to strike. The two men tumbled to the ground and rolled over one another.

"What the hell?" said Frank.

Bill laughed, but then strode over and put his gloved hand on the doorframe. He yanked it back fast. "Damn, that's hot," he said. The tall, blond fireman peered down at Frank and Jack on the floor. "How'd you know?"

Jack just shrugged. "I'm psycho, remember?"

He got up and pulled Frank to his feet. "Come on, they're down here," Jack said. Seeing their expressions, he added, "I heard something, okay?"

As the trio trudged down to the end of the hall, Jack glanced back at the unopened office door, took a deep breath, and blew it into his mask. *That's two*, he thought.

#   #   #

By the time Jack returned to the station, suited up, and made his way to the fire, there was nothing left but cleanup. Steam and smoke rose above the blackened, brick building above him as weary firemen laid out bodies on the wet pavement and zipped them into black bags.

The bodies of ten small Asian girls — none of them more than fourteen — were lined up on the street awaiting bags. The tattered and blackened remnants of their thin, filmy nighties lay plastered against their frail bodies, making it nearly impossible to tell where negligees ended and skin began.

Jack shook his head. *Horrible way to end such a hard life*, he thought. Then his eyes were drawn to the far end of the corpse row where a large crowd of firemen milled around, staring at three bodies. Nobody spoke, but none of them could turn away either.

Jack rushed over and pushed his way through the uniformed crowd. He stopped dead when he saw the burnt and bloody bodies of Bill Hogan and Frank Terelli.

"We could have used you here today, Lynch," said a familiar voice behind him.

Jack tore his gaze from the half-burnt faces of his friends to look at Chief Andrews. The chief's black face was covered in ash, making him look like an African shaman painted for a tribal ceremony. It would have been comical if not for the streaks running down his cheeks through the ash.

As Andrews explained how the men and girls had died, Jack looked away. He couldn't face the chief. But when he turned, his gaze fell on the row of bodies. This world was definitely not right and there was nothing he could say to make the situation better. But there was something he could do. It might cost him his marriage, but he had to change the past. He had to change his mind.

Jack Lynch concentrated on his day and located the moment it had all gone wrong. Just one little tweak and he could set it right again. Maybe not for him and Maria. But at least nobody would have to die this time.

# # #

"Lynch!" called the chief. "Lynch. Are you with us?"

Jack turned back to face the chief. His face still looked like a tribal mask of smoke and ash, but the streaks were gone. He looked up. Smoke and steam rose from the building and all the windows had been blown out on the top floor. Firemen milled around collecting hoses and replacing gear on the trucks.

But there were no body bags. The Asian girls sat in the back of several ambulances, wrapped in blankets. As paramedics checked for injuries and dressed minor wounds, he could see the girls flinch away from the touch of the men. *They were saved from two hells today*, he thought. *But the scars of both may never heal.*

Jack looked at the chief, who was still waiting for an answer. "Yeah," I'm here, chief. "Here and ready for duty, as usual. What do you need me to do next?"

Andrews closed his eyes and shook his head. "I don't get you, Lynch."

Jack started to argue, but the chief held up his hand. "I don't want to know. Just go help Terelli and Hogan store the gear for the trip back to the house."

Jack snapped to attention and saluted. "Yes, sir!"

Andrews cocked an eyebrow, but then returned the salute.

As Jack walked to the truck, he glanced at his watch. "Damn," he said. "Maria's plane just took off."

# # #

"This was a great idea, Frank," said Jack. He placed another stack of chips in front of him and waited for his cards.

"Yeah," said Frank. "Atlantic City will cure what ails you." He looked at his cards and frowned. Frank didn't have much of a poker face.

"No offense, Frank," said Jack. "My cure includes Maria at my side, not you." But then Jack smiled. He knew this was better than the other timeline.

"She's off with that Blaine guy again?" Frank took one too many hits and busted.

Jack nodded. His seventeen wasn't enough to beat the dealer either. After the dealer swiped his chips into the hole, he plopped another stack on the table.

"You want I should have someone talk to him?" said Frank in his best impression of a wise guy.

Jack laughed despite himself. Frank might look the part of the swarthy, Italian mobster with his thick, black hair and square-set jaw, but his delivery was pure Hollywood. He'd probably never even met a member of the mob.

"Actually," said Jack, "I think that would just make things worse. I need to work this out myself."

"When does she get back?"

"Next week," said Jack. He looked at his cards. Double aces. He flipped over the second ace and added another stack to the split. An eight and a nine gave him two promising hands. "Just in time for our next rotation. We won't see each other for two weeks."

Frank tried doubling but got a two and swore under his breath. "It's too bad your sixth sense doesn't work on your wife," he said as they waited for the dealer.

Jack sighed again. *It almost had*, he thought. "Yeah," he said. "She seems immune to my charms anymore."

The dealer hit twenty-one and swiped the table clean. Frank almost knocked his chair over as he got up. "Damn," he said. "I need to buy another hundred."

As the two men walked toward the cage, Frank grabbed Jack's arm. "So, tell me, Jack," he said. "How does it work?"

Jack raised his eyebrow as his mouth dropped open. "How does what work?"

They stopped next to the slot machines. From the scowl on Frank's face, Jack knew his innocent routine wasn't working. "You know exactly what I mean," said Frank. "How'd you know about the stairs yesterday? And the door? And where to find those girls? How does your psychic power work?"

Jack tried to dodge the question again. "That's just a joke," he said. "You know, Jack, the psycho fireman."

But Frank wasn't buying it. Not this time. He gave Jack his stern, kill-or-be-killed Al Pacino look, which was far more convincing than his wise-guy voice.

He'd made too many changes in the factory. It had been too obvious. "I'm just lucky, I guess," he tried.

Frank shook his head. "Tell me now or find a new best friend," he said.

It was a hollow threat, but Jack knew he had to give in. "Let's head to the buffet," he said. "My treat. We can talk there."

# # #

The two friends sat in a booth amidst a vast, garish dining room cordoned off into sections by gleaming, golden-lattice partitions. Frank tore a hunk of rib meat off with his teeth and spoke while chewing. "So, let me get this straight," he said, spraying sauce all over the table. "You can change the past?"

Jack picked at his chicken and mashed potatoes. "Not exactly," he said. "I can alter a decision I've made. Turn right instead of turning left. Stop instead moving forward. Stay at the firehouse instead of stealing off to see my wife."

"And that changes what's already happened?"

Jack nodded. "It's like dominoes," he said. As he talked, Jack began placing his casino chips on end like dominoes, setting up a single line and then a second, unconnected line that started near the middle of the first.

"Time moves forward like a line of dominoes falling," he said. "There's nothing we can do to stop it or change its course, right?"

"Sure." Frank nodded, although the furrows on his forehead said he only half followed Jack's explanation. It had taken Jack a long time

55

and numerous migraines to figure this much out. He flicked the lead chip and watched as the chips fell all the way down the line. The second line remained standing.

Jack re-set the chips. But this time he turned the middle chip toward the second line. "When I alter a decision," he said. "It changes the course of time — at least for the world around me."

Jack knocked the chips over again. This time the path changed, leaving the original back section standing while the previously disconnected line toppled.

Frank looked at the chips and Jack could see the dawning light of recognition in his friend's head. But it wasn't exactly the light he was expecting.

"Can we use this, this talent of yours, at the tables?"

Jack just stared at him. "What?" he asked.

"Can you help me win at cards?" asked Frank, taking his more usual direct approach. "Use your power to make me win instead of lose."

"You want me to cheat at cards?" asked Jack.

Frank nodded and then shook his head no. "It won't be cheating. It'll just be making the right choices...every time." A huge smile spread across his lips.

Jack stared at his friend. "I tell you I'm basically a superhero who can live through any fire and save every trapped person...and all you want to do is use me to make money?"

Frank nodded, still smiling. "Well, yeah!"

"Don't you want to know how many people I've saved? How I got this power in the first place? What it's like to be, be...Spiderman?"

"More like the Temporal Idiot," said Frank. He grabbed Jack by the arm and pulled him from his bench. "You can tell me all about that later. Right now, I want to win back my money. All of it; every cent I've ever lost at these damn tables."

Jack actually felt a little silly. He'd never considered using his power for his own gain. Sure, he'd saved his own life a couple of times, but he'd never gone back to choose the correct lottery numbers, or win a bet, or even pick the right pony.

It just seemed wrong somehow. Jack didn't exactly believe in God, at least not in the all-powerful entity taught in his Catholic upbringing. But something or someone had given him this power — granted it when he'd faced certain death — and he felt obligated to use it to save others.

But then again, maybe he deserved this. He'd saved more than a dozen people yesterday alone. Besides, a nice diamond choker would go a long way toward making things right with Maria.

"Okay," he said. His smile now matching Franks. "Let's do it."

#   #   #

After a few hours of trying various games, they landed back at the Blackjack table. They'd tried roulette first. With 35 to one odds they figured to win some big pots fast and then get out while they were ahead. But it seemed the drop of the ball depended on a lot more variables than just Jack's choice of a number. They lost five straight spins before moving on.

Craps was also a bust. The universe was apparently a lot more random than Jack's domino theory predicted. At Frank's urging, they tried Texas Hold 'em, to some success. But the constant shuffling messed him up.

So, they came back to Blackjack and its huge shoe of cards. At first, they both played, but Jack's altered decisions had hidden effects on Frank's hands.

After an hour, Jack was up twenty thousand. But his head swam with alternative histories of hands won and lost, making his temples throb and his vision blur. His migraines had returned, and he could hardly think straight.

He flipped a hundred-dollar chip to the dealer and stood up. "Let's cash out, Frank. My head is swimming."

"Oh man," said Frank. "Just a little longer. You can handle it. Ten thousand will just cover the 88-inch, 4K Smart TV I saw at Franklin Electronics. I need another couple thousand to upgrade to the deluxe home theatre package."

Jack rubbed his temples and concentrated on breathing. "You can have some of my share," he said. "I need massive amounts of Motrin and twelve hours of sleep."

He looked at Frank, whose shifting eyes showed he was torn between his friend's health and his dreams of a home theatre. Frank snapped his fingers. "I've got it," he said. "You just need to change one more decision."

"I don't want to put it all on one hand," said Jack. Remember what happened at the Texas Hold 'em tournament."

"No," said Frank. He guided Jack back to his seat. "Remember four hands back?"

Jack continued rubbing his temples but grunted his acknowledgement.

"You had a six and a five, said Frank in a hushed voice. "You hit and got a ten. You didn't need to change that decision, so we went on."

"So?"

"You didn't double down," said Frank. "You go back and double your bet on that hand, and we've got enough for my theatre, a diamond necklace for Maria, and maybe even a hot tub for the two of you."

"Fine," said Jack. "Then can I go to bed?"

Frank slapped him on the back. "Sure, buddy," he said. "I'll tuck you in myself and give you a kiss on the forehead."

"Some Motrin and a glass of water will be fine." Jack rubbed his temples as he concentrated on the hand Frank described. He envisioned himself doubling his bet instead of simply asking for a hit. A moment later, he opened his eyes.

#   #   #

"We need the seat, sir," said the dealer.

As the past rushed to catch up to Jack, he knew something was wrong. The crate of chips that had been sitting in front of him was gone.

"What the hell did you just do?" asked Frank from behind him. "How could you lose everything?"

"What?" asked Jack. "What happened?"

"There are people waiting for your seat, sir," said the dealer again.

Jack pushed himself to his feet and, with Frank's help, stumbled off the casino floor. In his mind, the last few hands reformed in his brain. He watched as hands he had won by making slight changes on hits and bets, go disastrously wrong. In the blink of an eye, they had lost twenty large, and there had been nothing Jack could do about it.

"What happened?" asked Frank again after he led Jack to a seat at the bar.

"I don't know," said Jack. "All of the changes I had made after that double-down hand reversed themselves. Once I made that change, I had no control over the other hands."

"Shit," said Frank. "The dominos fell the other way — all the way down."

It hit Jack at the same time. The past moved forward from the time of the change to the time he made the change. He had tried to alter a choice previous to another choice, and time had ignored the later changes. The dominos fell as they had the first time.

"I guess I shouldn't go back beyond my last choice," he said, more to himself than to Frank.

"Good tip," said Frank. Sarcasm coated his words like honey. "Let's remember that in the future."

#   #   #

"Another trip?" asked Frank.

Andrews had them on maintenance duty in the bay. Jack looked down from his perch above number nine's engine, oil stick in hand.

'Yeah," he said. "She just got back from her last trip, which lasted an extra week, and now she has to go right back. Some sort of emergency crept up after they left." He wasn't sure he believed it even after he said it out loud.

"An advertising emergency?" asked Frank. He tossed an oily rag up to Jack. "What? Did someone forget the jingle? It's not like anyone's going to die from an advertising emergency."

"Not to hear Maria talk about it," Jack said as he wiped down the stick. "'Heads are going to roll.' That's what she said as she repacked."

"I suppose Blaine is going as well."

Jack slammed the oil stick in, which bent almost in half. He tried to breathe away the anger as he straightened out the stick and slid it down to the end. "Of course."

"You should go kill that guy," said Frank. "And then just go back and decide not to kill him. At least you'd get the satisfaction of seeing his bloody corpse."

Jack jumped down and looked at his friend, trying to figure out if he was joking or not. "You're sick," he said. "Really, really sick."

Frank grabbed Jack around the shoulder and headed toward the tool bench. "Hey, no harm, no foul. Right?"

"I think I'll work out my marital problems without resorting to murder, okay?"

"Whatever," said Frank. "Just remember, I know a guy who knows a guy..."

The rest of Frank's clichéd repartee was cut off by the blare of the horn in the bay. Jack ran toward the lockers. Adrenalin coursed through his body, spurring him past Frank.

"Do you always have to be the first on the truck?" called Frank from behind.

Jack nodded his response. How could he sum up the rush he got from hearing the siren? Even as a kid that blaring wail set his blood on fire. He'd run to the scene and watch the firemen fight that primal force. The first time he'd seen a fireman carry someone out of a burning building, he knew he would be a fireman. He wanted to save lives.

That was what the siren meant to Jack — a chance to save lives. That's where the rush came from. That's where his power came from.

#   #   #

"Don't worry ma'am," Jack said through his mask between deep breaths. "I'll get you out of here."

Smoke billowed into the apartment from the hallway, coating the plastic-covered chairs and sofa in a layer of soot. He pulled the elderly lady

60

from her wheelchair and draped her over his shoulder. She was so frail he hardly even felt her weight. Spindly legs sticking out from polyester dressing gown under his arm were the only proof she was there.

"Terelli, Hogan," he called into his radio. "What's your twenty?"

"We're clear, Jack," came Frank's reply. "You're the last one inside."

"I've got an elderly female and am vacating the building," replied Jack. "Have paramedics standing by."

Jack grabbed an afghan from the couch and tossed it over her body before heading into the hallway. As soon as he reached the corridor, though, Jack knew he was in trouble.

Flames licked the walls around the elevator, which stood between him and the stairwell. While Jack had been searching, the fire had climbed the shaft to this floor. The fire was already devouring the dry, wool carpeting in the corridor, and it crawled steadily down the hallway toward him.

Jack double-timed it toward the stairs, hugging the far wall as he passed the elevator. Smoke curled around the base of the elevator door. Fire ran up the wall and dripped onto the floor around him as he ran.

Jack glanced down the middle stairwell. A red glow and dense smoke below told him he needed to move on. But smoke obscured the rest of the hallway as well. He crept forward, feeling the wall with his hands. It was warm but not hot.

The old lady began coughing under her blanket. Jack tore off his mask and placed it over her head. There was nothing to do now but make a run for it. He repositioned the woman on his shoulder and jogged into the smoke.

Tears immediately welled up in Jack's eyes. He tried to take shallow breaths, but the exertion of carrying the woman forced more and more smoke-laden air into his lungs. His chest burned but he had no choice but to continue.

Then Jack heard a loud crack and his stomach leapt into his throat. He had made the wrong decision. The floor fell away, and Jack plummeted into the blazing inferno below. Lying in a broken heap, his skin sizzling and his lungs filling with ash, Jack Lynch tried to concentrate on a point in time when he could have made a different choice.

#   #   #

"We're clear, Jack," said Frank in his ear. "You're the last one inside."

Confusion gripped Jack for a moment as he reoriented to his recent past. The sequence of events that led to his death lay before, and he knew what he needed to do.

"Get the ladder up here," he said into his radio. "I don't think the hallway is safe anymore."

There was silence on the other end for a moment before Frank replied. "You got a bad feeling about that, do you?" he asked.

"Yeah," said Jack. "Call it a premonition." He crossed the old lady's living room to her window and threw it open. Waving at the gathered firemen below, he said, "Up here boys. She'll need to be carried."

When Jack reached the bottom of the ladder, a chorus of cheers and applause erupted from the gathered firemen and bystanders. He placed the elderly lady on a stretcher and watched as the paramedics put an oxygen mask over her face and wheeled her toward the ambulance.

"Lynch!"

Jack turned to see Chief Andrews heading toward him. He half expected a public dressing down for wandering off alone inside the burning building, but the chief's normally stern face seemed oddly concerned. His eyes darted and his mouth quivered.

"What is it, chief?" he asked.

"There was an accident," Andrews said. He paused again and Jack began worry. "We just got called to the airport. All available rigs."

Okay," said Jack. "No problem. Let's roll."

Andrews placed his large, dark hand on Jack's shoulder and looked him in the eye. "I'm sorry, Jack," he said. "It was your wife's plane. The dispatcher saw her name on the passenger list."

Jack stared at the chief with his mouth hanging open. His arms felt dead at his sides.

"Is she...? Are there...survivors?" he asked.

The chief shook his head. "Stay here, Jack. Help with cleanup. "We'll send a car for you later."

Jack couldn't move. He nodded and stared at the chief's back as Andrews ran to the truck. Jack's entire body felt numb and cold, like all the heat had drained from him. He swayed and the world around him grew dark.

Frank grabbed Jack before he fell. He helped his friend to the ground and sat next to him.

"I'm so sorry, Jack," he said. "I'll stay here with you."

Jack came to a decision. He shook off Frank's arm and stood up, straightening his uniform with a jerk of his hands. "No," he said.

Frank scrambled to his feet. "I'm not leaving you, buddy."

Jack looked at Frank and smiled. "No. I'm not going to let her die. I'm going to change this."

Frank grabbed Jack around the neck with both hands. "It wasn't your decision, Jack. She left on the trip. You can't change that."

Jack shook his head. "She asked me this morning," he said. "She told me she would stay if I wanted. I just couldn't do it, not after how I... how she looked at me when I...."

Even though none of that last argument had happened, Jack would never forget how Maria had looked at him when he'd grabbed her and tried to force her to stay.

"I can't stand in the way of her career," he said at last, finding enough of the truth he could tell Frank to finish his thought. "She'd never forgive me that. So, I let her go."

Frank nodded for a moment and then said," Wait, Jack! You can't. You changed something in that fire. I know you did. That's why you called for the ladder. If you go back to this morning, the fire will play out as before. The dominoes, remember?"

Jack nodded.

"That woman will die if you go back."

Jack grabbed Frank in a bear hug. "No. We'll both die," he whispered. "Good-bye, Frank."

Jack closed his eyes and concentrated on his bedroom at five o'clock that morning.

\#   \#   \#

"Lynch!" yelled Chief Andrews. "Lynch. Get your head in the game!"

The world resolved around Jack. *What happened? Why aren't I dead?*

The remains of the burned-out tenement loomed in front of Jack as two different pasts fought for control of his attention.

Firemen and paramedics zippered up body bags over to one side. A feeling of dread came over Jack. He ran toward them as the new past replayed inside his head. He had told Maria not to go, which should have been the end of it. But that led a huge argument about her career, and Blaine, and his unwillingness to allow her to succeed.

He reached the row of bodies and scanned the black and brown faces; mostly old or incredibly young. Just what you would expect from a fire in the Projects. Healthy adults handle the smoke better than infants or the aged. How many had he saved the first time? He couldn't remember yet.

The fight played out much like the one from a few weeks earlier. In the end, Jack convinced Maria to stay so they could work things out. He told her he loved her. He told her he was afraid of losing her and that she meant more to him than life itself.

She had asked him if she meant more to him than being a firefighter. He told her she did. To save her life, Jack had lied, just a little bit.

Jack came to the end of the line and found her. She almost looked asleep, her gray hair tightly curled around her gaunt, ashen-brown face. But a blackened and tattered polyester dressing gown hid most of the burnt flesh beneath. She hadn't made it. But he had. Jack never made it to the fire because of the argument, and this woman — and many others — had paid the price.

"So that's it," said Jack. "A life for a life. That was the choice I made. That's the choice I have to live with."

He stood there for a moment before reaching up and removing the shield pinned to his shirt. Kneeling down, he placed the shield on the body of the woman he'd killed. He thought he should say something, but no words came. After a minute, he zipped the bag over her head and turned to walk home. ♜

A LOVE ALL CONSUMING

By Lewis Figun Westbrook

SHE'S BEAUTIFUL. THERE'S NO BETTER way to put it. Her skin, a delicate cream, so pure I want to dive into it. I trace my fingers across her and watch the way it ripples, like droplets into a still lake. Her hair is so dark I pretend I can see my reflection in it. I love the way it shadows her face, saying this is the brightest thing in the room. Her lips are plump, a cherry red that convinced me I had never kissed anyone worth kissing before.

Today is our one-year anniversary. We have the luxury of getting ready together.

I stand in the bathroom door as she flitters in front of the mirror. Her makeup routine consists of so many swishes and swipes that I cannot even see the consequence of, but I know the final piece will be glowing. I know no matter what she does, she will be stunning.

I switch between watching her reflection and her profile. Our mirror is older, black circles dot the corners like mold impeding on our vision. It makes her look more magical. More impossible.

She's impossible, and I am the luckiest person on Earth.

Her dress is a little red thing. Right now, it scrunches against her thigh, pulled up enough to see skin rare enough to be a treat. I want to place my hand there. To feel her warmth against mine. To hold her.

She turns to me, smile shining in a way that has nothing to do with the bright lipstick and everything to do with the reason why I love her. She cocks her head to the side, "You ready?" I let her lead me out the door.

We picked a tiny little place at the edge of town. They light candles at every table and vines drape down to give you a semblance of privacy. All of their desserts are bite-sized.

We walk there, and our shoes make completely different sounds. Hers is a tight click and mine a sort of slap. Her coat is long enough to reach past her dress to her knees and mine just lingers on my belt. I order the red meat, and she asks for a watermelon salad. The waiters wear white shirts with black aprons.

I tilt my glass towards hers. "Happy one year."

They clink, and something glints in her eye. "Here's hoping we make one more."

We fine dine the whole evening. We gorge ourselves on first-class platters. My meat runs red, and I sink my teeth into it. The steak knife has an elegant golden handle. The serrated edge pulls towards me. It feels too pretty to be deadly. It's made for warnings more than anything. Intimidation over follow-through. I can hear the crunch of her salad and the way her fork plunges through the greens. The melon juice dribbles down her jaw. When she smiles the grains of sugar glint in between her teeth.

By all accounts, it's a successful night.

We walk home in the cold. She wraps her arms around her body, and I pull her close. Her dress and jacket flap in the wind, and stray pieces of hair stick to her lips. She's full. She's gorgeous. The dark light hides her splash of freckles across her chin, but it lets her eyes glow like they are supposed to. It gives enough space for them to be the star of the show. She matches the night sky.

"This was wonderful. And it got me thinking." Her eyes meet mine. She gazes into my soul, and I think not for the first time that she sees me like no one else. She holds herself closer. Tilts her head up to the sky. The words come out just above a whisper. "There's one last thing I think we should do tonight."

The buzz from a couple beers shoots right to my head. Her hand is resting near my hips. "Absolutely." I nod without any further details. Anything with her will be wonderful. Anything with her will be perfect.

We barely make it into the door before she pulls me into bed. Her smile is a one-sided smirk. It pulls on the freckles like a changing constellation. She pushes me down onto the bed and straddles me, the smile only growing.

She leans in close, and when our lips touch, they explode. Every fiber of my being loves her, and they all react to her touch, to her presence, to her love. She controls me, and I lean into it happily. She pulls away just to kiss my cheek, then my jaw, then my neck. She creates an intricate trail to my ear and sinks her teeth in. With a little tug she lets go and smashes into my mouth. Her saliva mixes with mine, and the iron of my earlier meal drifts back up to my tongue. I can taste the watermelon too. All fresh and forgiving. Her one hand drifts behind her. It rests on my thigh and creates a direct line.

God, I'm so turned on already it's ridiculous.

She pulls back and places her hand on my chest. The pressure holds me still, and I find it hard to take my next breath. "You ready?"

It's deadly. It's all I can think about.

I nod first, the words catching in my throat. "Yes."

She leans down, starting with a soft slow kiss before she bites my lip. "Good." She pulls up and the iron splatters my tongue anew.

I've always hated the biblical talk, but she makes me think they got one thing right. I want to become one flesh with her. To be one flesh.

I grab her hips. I pull her closer.

She smiles, that red lipstick growing and smudged around her lips.

"Kiss me again. Please." I lean up as she leans down. We meet halfway, and we're both ravenous. My tongue explores her teeth, and her hips roll underneath my hands. The pressure on my lips is static, and I feel the tingle trail down my body. It's aching.

She's like magic. She adjusts so she can kiss along the line only ever increasing the pressure. She starts on my chest. Finds the most sensitive part of my stomach. Licks my thigh.

I let my hands move across her body in response. Biting into her anytime she does something edging on too good. It's all so good.

My attention focuses on everywhere she's touched. Everything feels more real when she interacts with it, like she alone could turn my skin on. Could give me a super power. It keeps buzzing even after she's moved on.

I kiss and nimble. I let my teeth drag against her skin. I listen to her moans and feel her push into my touch.

We know each other so well.

We flick the buttons and watch each other react. We thrive in them. In each other. Our clothes come off. Her body gets closer to mine. Our skin presses so close I think we could break each other apart. I think we could twist into each other. I swear we are so close to becoming one.

Our skin is turning moist, the sweat sticks to me. I pull away—

There's red on my hands. It's wet. It's not like lipstick. It's not just sweat. When I peel my fingers apart there are strings.

Blood.

It bottoms out my stomach. It's the iron already in my mouth. Her skin is in between my teeth. Her flesh is traveling down my gullet.

I've consumed her.

"Don't stop," she tells me. There's a moan in the back of her throat.

She's consumed me. The aches across my body unlike anything I've ever felt before make more sense now.

They don't feel like holes. She's taken a bite out of me, and all it did was make me feel more. She's stolen my heart. Might as well have my other flesh too.

I lick my lips. I find the taste again. Her. Me.

Flesh. Love.

I look down. There it is. The red mess across my body. We'll mix it with white soon. I can see the spongy texture of my own body. It's lighter than the blood making it shine through. It has specks of white, not pure or like sugar. A flesh white like pressing into your skin hard. I wonder if they have different textures. If you would notice it. If your tongue would care.

I wonder how many layers of skin I've already bitten through. It's just like biting a baby carrot. That's what they always say.

It's so much easier than I would have thought.

My lips have gone clean at this point. The taste lingers, but it's already fading. It's already so weak.

"Please." She pulls me against her body. I want another taste.

I bite her shoulder and hold her closer. I like the half scream that comes out of her mouth.

We don't stop.

As long as I can keep going I will.♜

ILL MET BY MOONLIGHT

By Frazer Lee

I BEGIN WITH CAUTION THIS disturbing tale, as it is not my intention to cause distress and tension in the male reader towards the opposite, fairer, sex. Unfortunately, a greater effect may result within the psyche of the female reader as my tale can only serve to illustrate that the idea of the monstrous feminine is much, much closer than one expects.

\#   \#   \#

It began with the moon. I remember it distinctly. I remember thinking it looked like a perfect slice of lemon floating in a glass of cold gin and tonic. This half moon transfixed me on that chilly night, much more than the entertainers who danced and cartwheeled their way through the cobblestones of Covent Garden. I stood rooted to the spot, gazing up at that moon, thinking if only earthbound sights had such power and beauty. Chasing memories of loves both lost and never attained from my cobwebbed memory I instead focused on the moon. Truly the most beautiful thing I'd ever seen.

Until her voice. A voice like diamonds from over my shoulder.

"She's looking back at you, you know."

Frozen, I was, and not from the cold. This voice was a sister to the moon that so held me. Undoubtedly American in accent, with the ponderous articulation of the West Coast and a tingling quality from some hidden tone or pitch that only certain night creatures could, probably, hear.

Turning slowly around, God and His angels put a face to that voice for me, and in an instant, I was utterly powerless. I remember every detail of her. Every curl, curve, shape, and scent. The visual information of her being penetrated and wrapped itself around my brain. Within my entire field of vision was her face, like a projection on a silver screen. When I blinked, I could see the afterimage of that half moon. I was hypnotized. Her eyes were sharp green and blue. She had long black eyelashes, and a noble poise to her bone structure. The gentle slope of her nose and cheekbones accentuated her lips, which seemed to me as shiny red velvet as they parted cleverly in a smile to reveal teeth of pure white. She licked her lips with a quick movement of her tongue and took a step toward me, curtseying.

"I am Christine Nimbo. From Washington. I'm sorry, but I too have a fondness for the moon and such. I hope you don't mind my breaking your concentration like this, mister…"

"Shaw. William Shaw. And I feel compelled to thank you for breaking my concentration. I believe it can be dangerous to look on such beauty for prolonged periods without the aid of a stiff drink."

My forwardness shocked me. But as anyone who has fallen in love in the blink of an eye will know, the human character is infinitely adaptable in any given emotional situation. That did not however prevent her reply from shocking me even more. Glancing around the piazza, this delectable Christine turned a mischievous eye back to me and said, "Where can we get a good stiff drink then, Mister William Shaw, as I too have been gazing at that blessed moon for too damn long."

Within two hours, over several glasses of very good port, I had learned all about Christine Nimbo from Washington. Her father had been ringmaster of a well-known travelling circus until falling in love with a local girl in Seattle who came to see the show every single night. Christine's father decided to marry right away, and tears were shed when his comrades learned he would not be accompanying them to their next port of call. The wedding reception was a spectacle with clowns, horses, elephants, and trapeze artists all celebrating their master's wedding in true carnival fashion. A feast was held in the Big Top.

Life became quiet when the circus left town, and Christine's father took the post of teacher of Mathematics and English at the local schoolhouse. His wife soon became pregnant with Christine, and they added an extra room to their small house in preparation for the arrival of their firstborn.

Their existence was idyllic for a while, that is, until the young father's wanderlust returned to him. The magnetic pull of the travelling circus teased his very blood and in his heart of hearts, he dearly wished to be back amongst his brethren, learning new dialects and landmarks. The map of his mind had formed boundaries when he arrived in Seattle. His agony was great as he watched his beloved wife and daughter grow colder towards him as he spent less time at home and more at the alehouse or walking alone in the woods. Soon after Christine's first birthday, the ringmaster fled his happy home in search of that which called to him. His wife, aided by the light of the full moon, searched for him in desperation amidst the trees and over the tracks and plains until the sun came up. She returned defeated, her clothes tattered and torn, the next morning and weeks passed before the locals could get a word out of her. Christine's mother had many admirers, but she never took another lover and stubbornly raised her daughter alone in near poverty. Fortune struck when Christine's mother was offered a post in the local schoolhouse as her knowledge of history and her good memory made her a suitable understudy for the ailing history teacher Mr. Vetch. Christine was therefore very well provided for and began to display the same keen, inquisitive mind as her mother and some of her father's curiosity.

It was with reluctance and pride therefore, that Christine's mother allowed her to travel to Europe to study and work in the multitude of fantastic cities she encountered. This decision was scandalous in the community at that time, yet to mother and daughter there was no question that Christine was capable of looking after herself. It was one year prior to her arrival in London that Christine was happily studying Spanish and making a handsome living selling flowers and coral to tourists in the bays of the Basque country. Christine received a telegram from the principal of the schoolhouse in Seattle telling her that her mother had died in a fire. The schoolhouse had burned down. Nothing remained of it, or her mother. Christine attended the memorial service and left Seattle quickly, as she found it hostile and changed. Her old school friends had become closeted, and they sickened her with their aprons and backyards and cries of "Settle down!" No, Christine still had the ache of the traveler in her belly and set off once again for Europe, this time arriving in Paris. She took time to lick her wounds and enjoyed all that marvelous city had to offer, spending hours in galleries and reading in the cafes of the Rue Saint Germain.

Having studied hard for a year and having accumulated considerable savings from her job as a florist in the Temple, Christine rewarded herself by moving on to London. She had never before experienced London's galleries, cathedrals and bustling street markets. Christine found this city to be a joy that sang to her heart. She took lodgings in Hampstead and became a godsend to her landlady Mrs. Harris, whose advancing years made it difficult for her to keep the house in order. Christine became as a daughter to her, helping out whenever she could, and scolding her for not taking a moment's rest, even when out of breath. This was to be Mrs. Harris' undoing, as one day she had a heart attack whilst bringing coal up from the cellar. Christine returned from an outing to find her cold and lifeless on the stairs. The funeral was a slight affair, as Mrs. Harris knew very few people and kept to herself. Her tenant had, however, become so dear to her in those final months that Mrs. Harris left the house and all her monetary wealth to Christine in a will written not two weeks before her demise. She considered selling the house, donating the money to several charities, before moving on to another continent altogether. Yet deep inside, Christine had reached a state of grace and serenity. All her life, it seemed, she had been plagued by abandonment and death but had remained resilient and brave throughout. She could not help feeling that her benefactor had left her exactly what she needed at this stage of her life. Calmly, and without any fuss, she set about decorating the house in her own style, with dried flowers and gifts from the sea, Indian fabrics, and church candles. Then she established a small florist's shop in the commercial row of Hampstead Village nearby.

"It's quite a story, no?" she said, drinking the last of her port and licking her sparkling lips as she set the empty glass down on the table.

"Good God yes," I replied earnestly, the sweet song of her voice still gently murmuring inside my head, "I feel I haven't lived listening to your story."

"Oh, you've lived all right, Mr. Shaw. Just not to the fullness of your potential, no?"

And with that, we kissed. And something changed forever in my heart.

I was working at that time as a clerk in a tailor's just off Regent Street. The owner, a fat, grumpy gentleman called Mr. Caplan, worked me like a dog. I was often given to wondering how business could be as bad as he always complained it to be when the pile of paperwork persisted to grow on the corner of my desk. Towards Christmas, the seasonal orders almost tripled and I found myself working increasingly long hours for, I might add, the same wages. I began to despair, as no sooner had I cleared the workload, an even bigger pile would appear as if by magic first thing the next morning.

Gradually I saw less and less of my beloved Christine. My lunch hour shrank to about five minutes and once, I had so much work to do that I forgot Christine was waiting on the doorstep below my office in the belief that we were to go to the pictures together. Somehow remembering as I finished for the evening, I grabbed my hat and coat and rushed downstairs. Thankfully, Christine had been put in a cab by the concierge of the neighboring Hotel Royale and sent home. The concierge was a giant of a man, rather like an iceberg in an overcoat, and he picked me up by my lapels and gave me a severe ticking off for my outrageous treatment of such a delicate flower as Christine. I rushed to her home, and although I could see smoke from the chimney and lights in her rooms, she would not acknowledge me. Unable to sleep, I arose from my bed and walked the great distance from my room in Bermondsey to Caplan's of Regent Street as the sun came up. I was in no fit state for work and my employer seemed to sense the trouble in my brain and the storm in my mood. By late afternoon, he had given me a modest Christmas bonus and told me to take the remainder of the week off. This only gave me an extra day's holiday of course, Mr. Caplan being no fool, but his generosity almost caused me to fall off my chair in shock and served to lighten my mood considerably. And as my mood lightened, an idea formulated within me. For the first time in ages, I felt as though my head and heart were working in tandem once more as when I had first met my beloved.

She let me into her house that evening. After my very unworthy self had devoured a superb meal, I sank to my knees and offered her the ring I had purchased on my way from the office. Her face was bathed in the firelight, and I swear she never looked lovelier than at that moment. Her eyes communicated such a profound mixture of joy and sorrow that I could not doubt earnest reply of, "Yes, I will marry you, Mr. Shaw."

Everything was as new again and we sat by the fire and talked animatedly over several glasses of our favorite port wine. Gradually, Christine moved our conversation from us, to me, to my job, to work in general. Transfixed as I was by her voice, I must admit that I became increasingly uncomfortable.

"The problem with all you Londoners is that all you do is work, no?" she said, "I mean you are truly obsessed with it. Work, work, work. I like to earn an honest wage, but life has so much more to offer. I've watched you losing your soul to a desk full of paper, Bill, and I don't like it, not one bit." She always called me Bill when she'd been drinking. Especially port wine. "I don't want my husband to be soulless to his wife, to his children," she said, "And so, I want you to leave your job and never go back to that horrible place."

"And if I don't? If I refuse?" I knew the answer. Utterly in her spell. Utterly in thrall of her. Utterly powerless once again.

"Then I won't... I *can't* marry you my love because gradually, I'll lose you anyway if I let you go on."

"But how will we live?"

"In paradise, my darling. You'll move in here and help me with the florists. We'll be a good team, no? It's settled then."

We filled our glasses and drank a toast to our happiness. I felt we were drinking to my death as a man. I even told her. She told me this was the typical male ego. I'm inclined to agree, even now. But in retrospect, I believe even so ugly a beast as the ego must surface on occasion, if only to preserve some kind of balance.

No matter. I did as she said and sent a resignation letter to Mr. Caplan. His honorable reply consisted of my final wage and a glowing reference, should I require one in the future. Christine kissed the frown from my head as I read it and said we should place it in a frame.

We decided upon a rural wedding and took leave of London to get married in my parent's village in Somerset. To my delight, my parents took instantly to Christine, and we rejoiced in an open-air ceremony in the shade of huge trees one midsummer morning. The Second World War loomed, preventing us from returning to London, and we took my parents' small guest house as a honeymoon cottage. As the war raged on, Christine and I stayed safe in our bed and our love amidst the trees of my youth.

My wife was never happier. She craved the fresh air and the windows in our humble home were rarely closed. Sometimes I awoke in the middle of the night to find her gone; a warm indentation in the mattress where she had lain. I would creep to the open window overlooking the vast weeping willow and birches of the garden and watch her spinning and dancing there. All the while she had her head thrown back and she embraced the stars and the moon as their light seemed to rain down on her, my beautiful wife, dancing barefoot in the garden.

One such night, it was raining heavily, and the roof had sprung a leak above our bed. I moved the bed to one side with Christine's help and placed a bucket beneath the leak to catch the water. The drip-drop of the rain was to me as the tick of a clock, and I was soon sleeping deeply. No such luck for my poor wife, who could not bear the sound, which conspired with the brilliant light of the full moon flashing and flickering through the rain clouds. A terrible migraine took possession of her skull, and she ran out into the river night without even closing the door. I awoke soon afterwards and instinctively crossed to the window, narrowly missing the bucket, half full with chilly rainwater. I peered out into the garden as I latched the window for fear it would blow open and strike me. I saw nothing save the rain pounding the grass. And a panic seized me.

Pulling on my greatcoat and boots, I ran out into the storm, crying out my wife's name. The ferocity of the wind robbed me of my words. From the garden I could see her footprints heading in the direction of the lane. The full moon had a cousin that night, in the sheets of lightning which further illuminated the empty space where my wife should have been, distressing me further. I stumbled down the lane and into a thicket of trees before coming to a halt in a small clearing next to a felled tree into which I had carved my name as a small boy.

I could hear breathing in the trees beyond. Crouching, as this seemed to improve my hearing, I concentrated on the sound and slowly moved towards it in this self-same posture with a quickening heart.

Eyes were watching me. Eyes like coals, hot and glowing, impervious to the cold and the rain. A low steady growl replaced the breathing and I stood erect, beginning already to retreat from this hider in the woods.

The beast erupted from the trees and tore at my greatcoat with huge white fangs, tearing a piece of my lapel away. Suddenly, the beast halted its attack and sat back on its haunches chewing the torn cloth slowly. I could see through my fear and the drizzle of my vision that it was a large wolf. Its eyes seemed very old to me somehow, like fossils encased in ice. Slowly, it chewed and sniffed before returning to its hiding place in the trees. I fought the paralysis that had taken me and somehow managed to turn and flee the terrible scene of my near-death. I ran and ran until I collapsed on my bed, fully clothed and soaking, numbed by the terrors of the wild and the disappearance of my wife. I battled with sleep but passed out in shivers and whimpers as the rain pounded deafeningly on the windowpanes.

Several weeks passed and there was no sign of Christine. My parents were distraught, and my mother grew sick with worry. We contacted the local authorities, but their searches proved futile. Christine had gone. Ripped from my life like a flower from its bed.

The rains returned and my melancholy became to me as permanent as a Siamese twin. The howling in my head upon her vanishing had levelled into a numb buzzing sound like angry bees. I had not slept for days, and food was unpalatable to me. I missed Christine with every fiber of my being. I was stricken without her. The sound of the raindrops in the bucket next to the bed on this cool, wet night served only at first to remind me of the events of that terrible night. Eventually however, to my inmost delight, the sound of the water dripping soothed me to sleep.

Soft, warm breaths on my face awoke me. I slowly sat up and the breaths moved away from me, as if knowing their work was done. Astonishment. As I opened my eyes, I saw my beautiful Christine, kneeling naked at the bedside. She had leaves in her hair, mud and moss caked her soft white skin. Her eyes sparkled with the wisdom and joy of a traveler who has finally returned home. My breath stopped in my throat as I reached out to hold her. Then I saw her hands. Covered in blood they were. Blood both dried and fresh. Tiny catgut strands of gore hung from her wrists like bracelets. And in her left hand, she held a piece of cloth. In Heaven's name, it was the lapel from my greatcoat, taken away by that massive wolf in the woods. Her eyes sparkled as if asking the question, "It's strange, no?" and I dropped my gaze to avoid those eyes, suddenly so terrifying to me.

I wished I hadn't looked down. For there, in the bucket of water next to the bed, I saw my wife's reflection, perhaps for the very first time. In the still rainwaters collected there, I saw the hot coal eyes and wolf face of my wife. Looking back to her, I could see she was placid now, but I knew in the quickness of my terror that this beast was within her and would come out again. Ashamed of what happened next, I am. But I have no regrets, even now.

My wife climbed onto my trembling body gracefully and whispered into my ear that everything was better now, that she had returned and would never leave my side again. Her words burned my brain, and her hot tears singed my flesh and we made love ferociously, over and over, like new lovers in their first heat. Me, a trembling mess of a man, and her at once beautiful and beastly, smelling of blood and meat and earth—and dead wood.

Christine's return was greeted with rapture by my parents; her absence explained away as a case of amnesia brought on by exposure. Certainly, my wife played the invalid, suffering visits from the family doctor and receiving silly gifts from my mother with the patience of a saint. But I could see her alertness behind those long lashes and heavy-lidded eyes. Something older and wiser than us dwelled in there. Reluctantly, my parents allowed us to return to London, my wife and I, back to the chaos, wreckage and strange peace left behind after the Blitz.

And so, I became prisoner to the beast woman whom I loved, in the idyllic surroundings of our Hampstead home. I knew that I could never leave, for fear that Christine would find me in her altered state one night as I ran and ran by the light of that bloody full moon.

Every moon cycle marked a little death for me. Although the periods in between my wife's transformation were filled with love and desire, I grew older and weaker as she remained young and strong.

I have been in this house for forty years now. Tonight is full moon and I have dutifully left the windows open for ease of exit for the beast. I am elderly, cold, and stupid. Today I found the reference letter from my old employer in a box in the cupboard. It says I am, "Loyal and trustworthy."

I dearly hope my wife, the wolf, remembers that when she returns. So greatly have I outlived my usefulness, I fear she may tear out my throat and take what meat remains on my old bones when she comes home through that window.

Funny, no? I can no longer see any beauty, *any beauty at all*, when I look up at the moon.♜

BY THE COLD OF THE MOON

By Liz Holliday

THOMAS CARTER SLIT OPEN THE last of the letters with his thumb. As he glanced at the single sheet of paper, his mouth tightened. He looked out of the kitchen window for a moment. The sky was full of low, rain-filled clouds, and he knew it would be cold up on the high fields.

He wondered if he should have sold the farm when he had the chance, perhaps got himself a nice soft office job. How many times had he thought that? He watched his wife, Jenny, as she ate breakfast at the simple wooden pine table that had been new when his grandmother was a girl. Her father sat next to her, reading *Farmer's Weekly*. The scent of drying herbs and fresh coffee overlaid the smell of burning wood from the stove. Even the dull early morning light could not wash out the rich colors of the red floor tiles, the smoke-blackened wooden beams. His Jenny in a labor-saving modern kitchen and her father in a home? No, he could no more sell out his family's two hundred years on the land than he could sell his soul.

Still, he'd be a fool to imagine things would get any easier. He sighed and threw the letter on the table. Jenny put her tea down and said, "Not more bad news, surely, love?"

"Bloody bank manager wants me in to discuss the overdraft." He pulled on his anorak. "First, we find lambs with sway-back. Now this."

Jenny's father put his magazine down. He scowled. "If you want a bit of help, you know you've only to ask. Money's there if you need it."

"Thanks, Dad," Tom said, "but you keep it. We'll get by, you'll see."

The old man's jaw worked. "As you like," he muttered and went back to his magazine.

Jenny stood up and got Tom's lunchbox. She snapped open the plastic lid and put an apple inside. "We'll be all right, won't we?"

"Of course, we will." Tom took the box off her. She was tall and no longer thin. The first delicate tracery of lines creased round her eyes and mouth. Laughter lines, he called them. How long since they had had a really good laugh together? But it did not matter, she was still his Jenny. He pulled her to him and held her close for a long moment. "Of course, we will," he said, as if repeating it could make it so.

#   #   #

Thomas went out into the yard and called his dogs, Megan and Jip, to him. Megan was getting old, he thought, as he rubbed her behind the ears. She liked the cold and wet no more than he did, but there was a ewe to be found that had been missing since the day before. Jip ran to the gate and back again making little, exuberant dashes here and there. He wasn't a bad dog, nor really stupid, but Tom found it hard to believe that Megan had ever been that silly.

When they had searched all the more likely places, Tom tried the old intake field, up by the woods. It was a rough bit of land, too hilly to plough. Tom's father had walled it round with the idea of pasturing animals on it. Then he watched as they sickened and died no matter what he did. Tom had been wiser. He let the land be, and though he had no profit from it still, it had taken nothing from him. He had a daydream that one day he would put caravans on it for the rich tourists up from London if he could get the planning permission. But running the farm took all his time, and there was never the money to put into any such wild scheme.

He thought of Jenny, with her other scheme, to take in tourists up to visit the dales. They could open up some of the spare bedrooms, perhaps convert the old barn. She would cook for them, maybe sell them her good jams and pickles. He imagined her fussing over them, making sure they were enjoying themselves. A right mother hen, his Jenny. He smiled. The thought of Jenny still did that for him. But then he thought of the bank manager, and Jenny who would be down in the village by now, working behind the counter at the subpost-office for Mr. Gleason. *Bloody southerner*, he thought. A refugee from the big smoke, he called himself. Foreigner, or as good as, the villagers said behind his back.

Tom came to the drystone wall of Old Fallowfield. He could see just by looking over it that the field was empty. Dispirited, he set off for home and second breakfast; there had been too many losses lately. But Jip caught a scent and chased off after it. He wriggled under the gate. Tom whistled him back. Jip checked for an instant, then ran on. Tom motioned to Megan, and she went after her wayward son while her master clambered over the gate. He saw Jip run up to the far wall, and then a little way along it. By the time he got there, Jip was nowhere in sight, but Megan was standing in front of a narrow gap in the stones. He pushed past Megan and went into the woods, gesturing for her to follow with a tiny movement of finger and thumb. She stayed where she was.

"Come on, old girl, let's get this over with, eh," Tom said, "Here to me, Meg."

She barked once, a sharp yip, then crept forward on her belly.

#   #   #

"Jip!" Tom called. "Jip!"

He threaded his way between the trees, drawn on by Jip's whimpering. Megan stayed close by his side. The whole place reeked of decaying mulch, and from time to time the breeze brought the smell of rotting meat from deeper in the woods.

"Reckon our old sheep's had it, eh Meg?" he muttered, though he was more concerned for Jip. By rights the dog should have come when he was called. He was silly, not disobedient.

"Jip!" he shouted again, "Jip!"

The young dog's whimpering grew louder. Tom pulled his anorak around him, against the growing chill. A glance at the sky told him that a storm was brewing. He hurried on, with Meg lagging at his side.

He came at last to a place where a tree had fallen, the trunk shattered from the stump and canted on the ground. His sheep was wedged into the space between the trunk and the bare earth. Black flies hovered above her dead body. Her eyes, opaque in death, stared at Tom.

He could hear Jip but not see him. Megan looked up at him inquiringly, and Tom pulled her ear gently. "Go on then, old girl. He's got stuck down some rabbit burrow. I'll be bound." He patted her firmly and pointed ahead. "See if you can't find him, eh my lass?"

Megan loped off. She cast about for a moment then made a little dash toward the tree trunk. She nosed at the dead sheep, growled softly, then left it.

Tom followed. His foot turned on something. He glanced down. A knot of feathers had stuck to the mud on his wellington, and on the hard earth a thrush's body had been reduced to a smear of blood and gristle.

He stepped over it. Megan was on the other side of the tree trunk. He could see her tail lashing back and forth and hear both dogs whining.

He went round the stump and saw that Jip was lying on the ground, hindquarters jammed beneath the tree trunk. At first Tom assumed he had been caught as the sheep had, by some movement of the trunk. Then he saw that the earth around the dog had been ploughed up. Jip's back legs seemed almost to be lying in a hole.

He crossed the clearing in two strides and went down on his knees by his dog. Jip growled softly when Tom touched him, but his tail lashed the ground weakly. Megan thrust her face between them, whining softly. Tom pushed her away. When she returned once and then again, he took her to the far side of the clearing and ordered her to stay.

He went back to Jip. "Hush, y'daft bugger, we'll soon have you out of this," said Tom. When he touched Jip's side, the dog yelped. Tom cursed, wondering if the tree had caused internal injuries.

A handful of hair came away in Tom's hand. He stared at it. The skin beneath was withered and dry, sunken in against the bone. It was like nothing Tom had seen before.

He decided he would have to get the vet to look at it when he got home. More expense. He got up and tried to roll the trunk off Jip. Megan lay on the far side of the clearing. She followed every move Tom made with her eyes, and she whined from time to time; but she was a good dog. She did as she was told and did not move.

The tree moved a little, then a little more. Tom grunted, wondering if he should go and get help. The wind picked up and a few splashes of rain wet his face. He decided to make one last attempt.

"Soon be home, old son," he said to Jip, and noticed with surprise how thin the dog was. The dog stared up at him with cataract-yellow eyes. Tom frowned, but then Jip moved his head and he decided it had been a trick of the light. Dogs bred from stock as good as Megan do not go blind at eighteen months. Yet he would have sworn that Jip had lost his sight. He shrugged. One more bloody thing to ask the vet about, one more bill to pay. Tom braced himself and tried to lift the tree just enough for Jip to crawl out of the way. It moved slightly.

"Get out of the way for Christ's sake," he shouted.

Jip stayed where he was, but the tree began to slide.

Tom could not hold it. He heard the tree branches scrape across the earth, and the wood of the stump tear. His fingers clawed at the rough bark, but it slid away.

He saw the trunk fall slowly to the earth. Jip tried to crawl away, but it was too late: the timber landed on his hind quarters. He yowled, but the tree was already rolling off him. It landed solidly on the earth and skipped once. There was a moment in which nothing moved, in which the only sound was Jip's terrible crying. Then the ground collapsed beneath the tree trunk.

For the space of a heartbeat Tom watched the earth sliding into the cavity that had been formed: dirt and stones and the tree trunk itself all rolling down into the cavernous dark that seemed to go on forever. Jip crawled forward, his paws scrabbling against ground turned treacherous. Tom moved to pull him clear, thinking vaguely about broken bones and the possibility of internal injuries; but before he could touch the dog, the wind began.

It seemed to spiral up out of the hole, bringing with it the stink of rotten meat and stagnant water. The trees were whipped by it, until their ancient heads seemed to dance in time to its keening.

He tried to grab Jip by his scruff, but the fur slid through his fingers, and the wind pushed him away. The dog cried out one last time. Then he slipped into the hole and was gone.

Tom screwed up his eyes against flying grit and the bite of the wind itself, but even so it seemed to him that there was a darkness at the core of it, something that no amount of blown dust could account for.

Almost as he thought that, the wind dropped. He trudged off toward Megan.

They would need ropes and tackle. Even then, he didn't think there was much hope for Jip, the hole was that deep. Megan got up as he approached. She tried to dash past him, but he called her to him. Her ears went flat to her head. Reluctantly, belly to the ground and tail down, she came.

He had not gone two steps further when a gust of wind like a closed fist shoved him to the ground.

He lay with his face in the mulch, tasting the rotting leaves. The wind died slowly down. He tried to clamber to his feet, but he ached as if he had been pummeled. While he was still on his knees, the wind began again. But it was different now. It became his lover, trailing careless, gentle hands across his body, kissing his mouth with utmost tenderness. And, like an ardent lover, it refused to let him go but babbled sweet nonsense in his ear. Almost, he could understand it. It promised a future full of ecstasy, if only he would say his name.

Such a little thing, it begged. Just your name, and in return an infinity of pleasure.

And though he resisted the seduction with thoughts of his home and wife and family, in the end he spoke the words: *Thomas Carter.*

"Ah," said a voice in the wind. "Now you have given yourself to me.

By your name I know you, Thomas Carter, and own you. By your name, you shall do what I cannot do, walk where I cannot go, strike the blow I cannot strike. By your name."

Tom tried to struggle to his feet. "I don't understand," he muttered; but most of him was numb with incomprehension. *Talking to the wind*, he thought. *I'm just talking to the wind.* He wondered if this was madness, or just its beginning. *Stress*, he told himself, firmly. *Just stress.* But still, he could not stand.

"See," the wind mocked him, "See what you will become." Tom managed to roll over and then to sit. He covered his face with his hands for what seemed a very long time. When at last he took them away, they seemed older, etched with lines and fleshless. He turned them over. The joints were knotted like old rope, the skin as fine as parchment. Terrified, he touched his face. It felt like a skull covered in thin leather, all sunken hollows and sharp ridges. He looked again at his hands, and as he watched, they withered and darkened. His joints ached, as though all the hurts he had ever feared had visited him at once. His sight faded as his eyes filled with rheum. At the last he saw his skin fall in tattered shreds from the ivory of his finger bones.

"Death will come for you, as it has now," said the voice, as Tom lay in the darkness, "And dust, and nothingness. The days of your death shall outnumber the days of your life, and in the end, it will be as if you had never lived. Your name will be forgotten upon the land, and all the works of your hands with it. Such is the lot of humanity, as it was in the beginning and ever shall be."

Tom whimpered in his mind. He had no throat to make the sound. "Do not cry," said the voice, "I have come, to save you. Only perform one task for me. Then death and the darkness shall never have you."

"What must I do?"

"Only kill this woman, and you will live forever, and be first amongst my Blessed Ones."

Tom looked, though he had no eyes to see.

"Jenny," he said, "You'd have me kill my Jenny. Well, I won't do it, and that's that."

"Very well, Thomas Carter. You may go."

Tom opened his eyes. He hurt. When he stood up his body was as bent as a question mark. He took one step forward, and then another: tiny, old man, pigeon steps.

"I'm only forty-two," he cried out, "What have you done to me?"

"Nothing time will not," came the reply, and laughter followed it.

"Don't. Please don't," Tom said.

"If you do this, you need never fear death, Thomas Carter," the voice said. And Tom knew it was true, for his body was suddenly young. More, it was perfect, strong, and beautiful; and he knew in his heart that this body would never die. He felt as if he could reach out and brush heaven with his fingertips, hold out his hand and cup the earth within it. He shone with the light of the perfect creation.

But the voice went on, "Or you can displease me. Then I will bring you death. But not death as others know it, which is merely the dissolution of the senses, the turning of the wheel—"

Thomas became old and died in an instant. Every part of him yearned towards the light and despaired for that which he could never know. "—no, I will bring you death that lasts ten thousand years, and in every second of it you will remember what you have lost, the glory that could have been yours."

But I'll have saved her, if nothing else.

The voice seemed to catch the unspoken thought: "Oh she will live a few more years, but what are they to the millennia of your torture? And there will be no heroism in this, Thomas Carter. She will never know what you have done for her. And you will know only the final futility of being human."

"But I'll have done the right thing," Tom said. "There'll be that."

"Yes. For ten thousand years of misery, there will be that."

"Why?" He muttered. Then louder, "Why must she die?"

"So that the witch who will imprison me a thousand years from now will never be born! For she will be in direct line of descent from this Jenny, and her power will be great. Yet the net she has woven and will weave is not perfect. In this time and place it is most loosely made. So am I able to find one vulnerable person, to bind him to my will. Thus, here I will ensure that

Jenny dies, and so the net unravels itself through time. And I will walk the earth in glory once again."

Tom lay silent.

"You do not understand. It is of no importance. Kill the woman and live, Thomas Carter. Fail and die. That is all you need to know. Now go."

"I won't. I won't," Tom screamed. He felt as if his brain were made of ice.

Thinking came hard, but at last he said, "If it's our children you're afraid of, kill me. Kill me. Don't make me do this."

The wind laughed in the treetops. He had said something stupid, but he couldn't see what.

"Thomas Carter, if she lives, Jenny will mother the line that will bring about my downfall. But I never said you would father it."

"My Jenny wouldn't do such a thing—" Tom said.

Laughter mocked him. "Your Jenny? *Your Jenny*? Haven't you had enough pain for one day? Must I show you?"

"No," he said. "No."

There was silence. Nothing moved. *I can't do this*, Tom thought; and he did not know whether he meant resisting or killing Jenny. And still the silence went on, and he could not move and could not stay, could not resist, and would not capitulate.

"Why me? I love her," he said at last. His voice was blurred by tears.

"A weapon easily made may break when the first blow is struck. Your heart is made of darkness, Thomas Carter, though you do not know it yet. From it I will forge a weapon that will strike hard and true."

"Wait. Let me think." But he knew his answer: the darkness was there, waiting for him to uncover it. "I'm not bad, I'm not," he whimpered. But he could not face the thing the voice laid out before him; and even as he spoke, he knew that the weakness in him was no different from evil, a core of darkness in his soul.

He did not speak again, but the voice did, "So. You have chosen well. By your name Thomas Carter, I bind you. By my name, am I also bound."

Tom felt his body grow slowly younger, until he was once more merely middle aged.

"But what is your name?" he asked, not wanting to hear the reply.

"I have had many names," said the voice. "Look in your holy books."

Tom screamed then, and beat his fists into the soil, but the voice was silent.

#   #   #

He was in the kitchen when Jenny came home. A mug of tea was going cold on the table, which was littered with felt tip pens and postcards.

Jenny shook the rainwater off her umbrella and left it in the corner to drip. "You're home early, love," she said. She seemed much more cheerful than when he had gone out. There was more color in her cheeks, and her eyes shone. He had not realized she enjoyed her job that much.

"Weather turned foul about two o'clock," he said shortly. "Anyway, I've had a bit of a problem. You might want to put this up in the shop window for me."

He handed her one of the cards he had written out. A look of surprise crossed her face as she read it. "Jip lost, love? Whatever happened?"

"I don't know," Tom said. He thought of the wind whipping through tree branches. "I really don't. One minute he's with me, the next he's off, and no amount of calling will get him back. I shouted myself hoarse, and not even Meg could find him."

"He might be stuck down a badger sett," Jenny said. "Do you think you should get up a search party? It'll be dark soon, with all this rain."

"No!" Tom said. He thought of voices calling him in the dark. He thought of dying. But that was nonsense. He was only forty-two. "No, if he'd been in that wood, I'd have found him all right. He's got a scent and gone off after it, mark my words." He licked his lips, thinking of a hole deep in the earth. He had lost a sheep there. That was all. "Pick of the litter I gave Pete Rogers for the stud fee," he said forcefully. "And it isn't my Meg that's the wrong 'un, I'll tell you." He banged the flat of his hand on the table. Tea slopped out of the mug.

"Never mind, love," Jenny said. "He'll come back. You'll see." She laid her hand on his shoulder.

Tom flinched.

\#   \#   \#

"Don't you want your dinner, love?" Jenny asked. She stood close by Tom, the aroma of baking almost masked by the scent of the expensive perfume he had bought her for her birthday. He could not look at her, at the bags like bruises beneath her eyes, so dark against her sickly pallor.

It had been eight days since he had come back from the woods. Since Jip had — since Jip had got lost. Eight days in which he had hardly slept, or spoken to Jenny, or touched her. He wondered if she had begun to hate him yet.

He refused to think about that and pushed the willow pattern plate away. Peas swam in rich gravy, next to an island of pastry. It made him sick to look at it. "No," he said, and stood up.

"Let me help—" she began.

"There's nothing you can do."

"Oh Tom. Don't. If it's the bank that's worrying you, maybe Mr. Gleason will give me some more hours at the shop—"

"Mr. Gleason, Mr. Gleason. I don't want to hear about Mr. bloody Gleason." That was it, he thought. The perfume wasn't for him. *The child is hers, but you are not the father.* He felt the muscles in his arm begin to move, knew that in one more moment he would hit her. Then, however things worked out, he would have killed something. He bit the inside of his lip so hard blood dribbled into his mouth. The pain brought him back to himself. "You shouldn't have to work at all. This farm should be our lives."

"Just for a while, love. Till we get straight." Her mouth smiled, but not her eyes. She stepped towards Tom. In a moment she would be holding him. It was more than he could stand.

"No!" he said, louder than he wanted to.

"Don't shout love. Dad'll hear, and you know how upset he gets—" Jenny put her hand on his arm.

90

"Don't touch me." He pushed her away. Her eyes went wide. He ran from the room. The door slammed behind him, punctuating the sudden silence.

#   #   #

That night he dreamed of lying in his grave with the cold clay all around him. There was a silence deeper than any he had ever known, silence unbroken by the small noises of the body, the rush of blood and the beating of the heart. He tried to speak. His mouth formed the word "Jenny", but no sound came. He would smother in such silence.

He strove upwards and broke through the binding earth.

She was waiting for him, girlishly slim and beautiful. "You have to die for me," she said gently. She kissed him. He responded urgently, pulling her hard against him.

He slid one hand inside her shirt, caressed the soft firmness of her breast.

He wanted to tell her that he loved her. He tried to break away from the kiss, but she would not let him. Suddenly, he could not breathe, and in that moment, he knew that she was stealing the life from him.

"No!" he screamed, "Jenny."

He opened his eyes. Her face was huge above him. Her hands reached out for him. She would kill him. He pushed her hard in the chest. She fell back across the bed. Tom scrambled up. He began to back towards the door, never taking his eyes off her, as if she were a dangerous animal.

Somewhere in the darkness, a dog barked. *Jip?* Tom thought. But it couldn't be Jip. Jip was dead, in a hole in the woods. So, it was a fox, or some such. Unless it was Jip.

To me, Jip, Tom thought.

The sound came again from further off.

"What was that?" Tom demanded.

"Nothing," Jenny said. "A fox, maybe?"

"No," Tom said. "It's Jip. It's got to be —"

"I don't think—"

"Don't cross me, woman," Tom said. If it wasn't Jip, then he was dead in the woods. But if it was him, then what Tom remembered was wrong, and he knew what he remembered...

Jenny sat up, rubbing her chest gently. Tom's tongue worked across his lips. He reached behind him and pushed open the door.

"Tom, love, do tell me what the matter is," Jenny said. "We can get help, the doctor or someone..." She stood up.

"Don't you come near me," Tom said. His voice shook.

"I wasn't going to," Jenny said quietly. She was angry with him, Tom thought. As if she had reason to be! A muscle under his eye jumped.

"I'm going to make a cup of tea," she continued, "So if you'll do me a favor and let me past—"

She pushed by him onto the landing. Her shoulder touched his chest. He pressed himself into the door jamb. "You mustn't touch me," he said. *How can I kill you if you touch me?*

"Oh, don't be so stupid."

"You don't understand!"

"No, you're right, I don't, and since you won't explain what's wrong, there isn't much chance I ever will. Is there?"

She was standing next to the head of the stairs. It would be so easy to push her... She would die. He would live. He knew he would never do it.

A door clicked open behind Tom. He felt trapped, knew he had to get away, had to try to think things through a bit.

"What the hell's all the shouting about, then?" It was Jenny's father.

"It's nothing, Dad. Go back to bed," Jenny said.

"Nothing?" Tom shouted, "I'll show you nothing!"

He went towards the stairs but crashed into the newel post to avoid her reaching hands. The carved acorn at its top slammed into his chest. He grunted. Jenny grabbed his arm. Unbalanced, he slipped down one step, then the next two, pulling her with him.

"I told you not to touch me," he screamed, and shoved her away from him, down the stairs. He fell awkwardly on top of her. His head crashed against the bannister, and his left arm folded beneath him. He heard soft, slow footsteps behind him. He twisted round, ignoring the pain, and saw the old man coming down the stairs one step at a time. He pushed himself up on his good arm. Jenny lay at the foot of the stairs, arms and legs twisted at awkward angles. Her eyes were open, but he could not see if they had rolled up or not.

Tom coughed. Blood dribbled out of his mouth. He got the front door open. Cold moonlight leached the front yard of color. As he walked out into the night, he thought he heard the old man — surely it was the old man — sobbing, and whispering Jenny's name, over and over again.

#   #   #

He woke to darkness and the sound of the wind weeping in the tree branches. The stars glared down at him. He lay on his back watching them, while leaf mulch soaked into his jacket. The wind sobbed with the voice of death. He remembered pain and stumbling to the edge of the woods. There had been the sound of sirens in the distance. After that, nothing.

"Oathbreaker. You are an oathbreaker, and forsworn. I have your name, Thomas Carter. Be warned, I shall take my forfeit. For though I was just, never was I merciful, nor shall I be so now..."

"She's dead. I killed her. What more do you want?"

The wind's icy fingers explored Tom's face. He turned his head aside, as the voice spoke again. "You are wrong. I tell you, Thomas Carter, your wife lives. For that you shall be punished. And in the end, you will do as you have pledged."

Relief thundered through Tom. "I won't."

"You will. I will not be baulked. Fail me, and you will feel my hand heavy upon you. This I have pledged, and I will not be forsworn."

Tom felt his flesh grow old, begin to putrefy, and slip from his bones. It was more than his mind could bear.

"Ahh," said the voice. "It is as I thought. I was too kind before, too merciful. You do need to see, that you may believe."

A vision came to Tom then: his Jenny in bed with a man. Not himself:

someone younger, dark haired. She moaned beneath her lover, legs up around his back, hands clawing his shoulders rhythmically as he moved. Tom screamed. His back arched. He strained upwards, as if galvanized by an electric shock. He wanted to weep, though he had never been one for crying. Tears would not come.

"No!"

"Oh, I tell you, if you let her live, this woman will betray us both, Thomas Carter. Think on what I have said, on what you have seen, and then do what you must."

Tom pulled himself up, shaky as a newborn lamb. He took one stiff-legged step, then another.

"I will make myself plain. Your body is dead, but you will live in it until you do my bidding. Then I will reward you, as I pledged. Fail me and not even death shall bring respite. Thus, are you bound, Thomas Carter, by your name. Thus am I, also."

Then there was nothing, only the wind in the trees. The dead man rose up and walked home.

#　　#　　#

The lights in the cottage were warm and inviting. There would be a fire in the hearth and tea on the table. Sometime during the evening Jenny's father would ask when they were going to start a family. Jenny would shake her head and say, "Oh Dad!" and smile in that way she had...

Tom imagined it all clearly. But when he looked down the valley, it was as if he were looking through a curtain of gauze. Night sounds drifted up to him on the breeze, and somewhere he thought he heard a dog barking, but he barely heard them.

Not mad, he thought, *not mad. I am merely dead.*

#　　#　　#

The scullery door was locked. Tom opened it and slipped inside. Megan whined from her place in the corner. He quietened her. It was a shame, he thought, that she was so old she was allowed to sleep indoors. A shame any of them had to age. He would spare his Jenny that, for her crime of betraying him.

He went to the knife drawer and picked out his skinning knife. It had belonged to his grandfather, and his grandfather before that, and the bone handle was worn smooth with age. He unsheathed it. The blade glinted like ice in the moonlight. He tested it against his thumb. He felt the flesh part, but there was no blood. No blood, no sweat, no spit, or tears. It was as well. He would have wept if he could.

He went into the dark hall. A line of light bled beneath the front room door. Waiting, he heard voices. It was difficult to make out words when his ears felt as if they were plugged with wax. He listened hard.

A man's voice said, "It will be all right in the end, love. Perhaps you should go to bed..."

He had heard that voice before. *Long ago*, he thought, *when I was young...*

In the village? Had he heard it in the village? He couldn't place it, couldn't think. There was only the knife, hard and cold in his hand, and the certain knowledge of betrayal and what of what he must do.

Jenny spoke too softly for Tom to hear.

"Bitch." His voice grated in his throat.

It took all his strength to push the door open, so that he knew death had made him weak. He went in anyway to confront his whore of a wife and her lover.

Jenny was sitting on the settee with her head in her hands. There was a man in the chair next to her. She turned to face Tom as he entered.

He took one pace across the room, two. Another stride and he was next to her, pulling her hair back with one hand while he stuck the knife in with the other.

"Dear God, Tom." The voice came from behind him.

There were hands on him. They were stronger than he was, younger than he was. He was sure of that, yet still he managed to throw them off. Furniture crashed behind him; there was a sharp grunt of pain, and then the

95

noise of a telephone dial turning.

He ignored the sounds, ignored everything except the knife and Jenny staring up at him with frightened eyes.

His Jenny. For a moment he wondered what he was doing. His Jenny, frightened of him, and Jip turning to dust in his hands, and ten thousand years of dying, and Jenny staring up at him — at her lover, her lover...

His Jenny. His Jenny. His Jenny. Blood fountained over his hands, hot and sticky—something in the world changed. He felt it, as if time had stopped and then began again—and his body spasmed. He stabbed down a last, convulsive time.

"The police, dear god get the police up here. He's gone mad, mad..." the voice came from behind him, but it trailed away in the moment that he recognized it as his father-in-law's.

Jenny, he thought, and fell to his knees. He felt the old man's hands pulling him away. He twisted around. His father-in-law stared at him.

Lines of anger and spite were deeply etched on the old man's face. They had not been there before. Tom knew it, just as he knew that his own body had been made young again in the moment of Jenny's death.

"My God, what have I done?" Tom whispered, but no tears came. He looked at Jenny. Her eyes stared up at him, flat and grey as a rain filled sky. Her lips were twisted into a silent scream. Tom bent, and pressed his own cold mouth against them, as if he could breathe life back into her.

The old man walked over to the settee. He stared down at his dead daughter.

Tom felt the first scalding tears and said, "I don't know what happened, Dad, I don't. I'm sorry."

But his father-in-law just stood in silence. When at last he looked up, the anger had gone out of eyes turned cold and hard as the moon. "I told her you'd hear about her and Mr. Gleason sooner or later-"

"No!" Tom shouted.

He pushed past the old man. His body was new-made, quick and strong. Jenny's father could not stop him. No-one could. He ran out into the brilliant night and ignored the wind as it jeered at him.

BY THE COLD OF THE MOON

#   #   #

Tom sat in the dark, up on the hill. The lights of the village were spread out before him, like a necklace on a jeweler's tray. Behind him, the wind blew through the night wood, speaking words he refused to hear. The police would not take long to find him. He was not dead. He thought he might be mad. But the old man's eyes had been hard, hard as he had never seen them before.

"Why?" he screamed aloud. "Why, if nothing's changed?"

"Ah, but all's changed, Thomas Carter," whispered the breeze, "I am free. Before, though the people sometimes lived in darkness, they strove mostly for the light. Now, though they may live in the light, they will work always towards the dark. You saw the old man, how he delighted in her death."

Delight? Thomas thought. Was that what he had seen? Perhaps. Or was it anger, hurt, betrayal? Again, perhaps. Thomas found he had no way of telling, nothing human in his heart to read the old man by. "He will find me," said the wind. "Others will. I will pleasure myself upon them and grow strong. Oh, you are Blessed indeed, Thomas Carter, for I am well pleased with you."

The wind caressed Tom, stroked his living flesh, ran its fingers lightly through his hair. He sat as unmoving as stone in his perfect body, watching the village lights. He felt as though he could send his senses spinning out across the world, and read each secret thought, watch each private action.

He felt like God, in his young body that would never age. For a moment he exulted in it. It was not weakness, and if it was evil, he did not care. He would live forever, find a thousand Jennys to answer all his needs.

And yet the weakness in him brought her face before his eyes: her greying blonde hair and blue eyes, and the blood that spurted over her face. He thought he heard her laughing somewhere beyond the wind and knew he had to join her...

The knife hung loosely in his fingers. He felt the bone handle, felt the weight of years it brought with it, all the good men and women, living and dying on the land.

He placed his arm across his knee. There must be no mistake. He laid the blade against the delicate flesh of his wrist and tried to push down on it. But he was weak. He could not force himself to apply cutting pressure. He willed himself to do it: willed the blood to well up around the blade, and the pain to lance through him and prove that he was still human.

The blade turned aside, as if the common skin and flesh and bone that Thomas was made of was somehow stronger than it. The handle of the knife was slick with sweat. It slipped in Thomas's grip. He held it more firmly, and this time he tried to drive it point first into his wrist.

Again, he failed. His skin went white where the knife pressed against it, but that was all.

Tom made an odd, mewling sound deep in his throat.

He looked down at the perfect, unflawed flesh of his wrist. He wanted Jenny, wanted to be held. To be safe. To live in a world where there was sense and order.

There was no safety, no sense.

He wondered if Jenny had forgiven him. He believed she had. More than anything, he wanted to join her, or to know nothing at all. There were other ways of killing himself, but he knew that trying them would be a waste of time. Death had kissed his lips and made his body immortal. There was no point testing his courage further. He already knew he was a coward: he had the memory of Jenny's dead eyes to tell him that.

And so, he sat in the star-punctured night, with his knife almost forgotten at his feet, and he listened to the wind moaning in the trees.

After a time, he heard a car stop on the road below. As the police led him away, he heard the wind speak to him: "I will not be forsworn, Thomas Carter. Now and forever, you are mine."

And in his perfect, eternal body, Thomas Carter wept. ♜

LOVE GUN

By Tom Waltz

IT ALL STARTED—HELL, IT all *happened*—because my girlfriend forgot her damn fake ID. I shouldn't have been surprised. I mean, she was always forgetting things—her house keys, her homework, her gym clothes... my birthday. Sheesh! And they say us guys are bad. Still, when she'd told me she'd forgotten it, I got pretty upset. Hey, when you're sixteen years old, and it's Friday night, and you're ready to party, little things like a fake ID become priceless. And besides, it's not like we could have gotten away with it if I had my own fake ID; I looked sixteen, no matter what the identification I handed to the cashier might say. Angie didn't. It's amazing how a little make-up can transform a teenage girl.

"Are you sure it's not in the bottom of your purse?" I asked, knowing it was hopeless. We were sitting in my old, beat-up '72 Chevy Impala—"The Boat" as my friends called it—in the liquor store parking lot. It was mid-October, a crisp time of year in the Midwest, and The Boat's windows were already fogging up from our breath—Angie frustrated, searching in vain for her ID, me huffing out disappointment.

"I told you, Mark, it's not here!" she whined. "I must have left it on my dresser. God, I hope my mom doesn't go into my room and find it. She'll kill me! You know how she is."

Angie's untimely death at the hands of her overbearing mother was the least of my concerns; there was drinking to be done and the only thing getting wasted was time. "Why don't we just drive back to your house and get it?" I asked.

"Oh sure, Mark, that would look real good. It was hard enough getting out tonight as it was, let alone going back." She pulled her hands out of her purse, sat back in the passenger seat, crossed her arms, and pouted. "My mom's so suspicious, she'd probably think I was coming back because I forgot birth control or something."

"Well, don't worry, *I* didn't forget that," I said, patting the wallet in my back pocket. The comment was an intentional jab at Angie's teenage senility.

"Screw you," she hissed under her breath.

Yeah, I hope so, I thought. *But first I want beer.* I wiped away at the condensation on the windshield.

"Hey, I know that guy," I said, pointing through the area I'd cleared toward the man standing just outside the liquor store's front door. "Well, I sorta know him. His name's Steve Campbell. Went to school with my stepsister Janice. I'll bet we can get him to buy for us. He's probably cool."

In a small Midwestern town like ours, you couldn't be too careful about who you propositioned to illegally purchase alcohol. Word got around and asking the wrong person for that kind of help was as bad as confessing to your parents. Of course, my mom and stepdad probably knew all along that I was out boozing it up most weekends; they just pretended they didn't. Angie's mom, on the other hand, still held on to the delusional belief that her only child was an innocent angel, and if she found out otherwise, well…

Funniest thing of all was the fact that none of the local store owners had ever told Angie's mom that she had a fake ID; we'd used the thing plenty. I figured they were just happy to get paid, and Angie, like always, had probably forgotten to consider the possibility of them ratting her out. I didn't remind her, though. Why mess with a good thing?

"I don't know, Mark," Angie whined some more. "It's too risky. Let's just go find the others and see if they've got extra…"

"Forget that, Ang," I interrupted. "Kyle and Lisa got other plans tonight, if you know what I mean." Kyle and Lisa were our best friends. "Kyle's mom and dad are gone for the weekend, and he told me that Lisa and him are gonna celebrate their six-month anniversary at his house. Alone." Actually, he'd told me that he'd kick my ass six ways to Sunday if Angie and I showed up, but male pride wasn't about to let me tell her that I took Kyle's threat seriously. "Anyways, I'm almost positive we can trust Steve. He's an old jock, and you know us football guys look out for each other. Just like me and Kyle always do."

I knew Steve Campbell used to play because he'd been an all-league cornerback in his senior year of 1978, the last year our school had a league championship season. You couldn't miss his picture displayed in the coach's office in the locker room, an old black and white job cut out from the county newspaper, with Steve standing next to Pete Martin, the all-everything quarterback from the same team. Kneeling in front of them, grinning from ear to ear, was Coach Duane Payton.

"Let me at least go ask him if he'll do it," I said, already opening my door. "If he says no, then we'll figure something else out."

"Whatever," Angie grumbled, frowning, her arms still crossed.

I rolled my eyes and closed the door, immediately forgetting about Angie's attitude. Thirst, after all, was on my mind. I walked over to where Steve stood. As I got closer, I could see that this was definitely the guy from the locker room picture.

He was about my height, maybe five-foot ten or so, with the same straight, shoulder length hair he'd had in the photo. The only difference now was the amount of forehead that was showing. He had on round, John Lennon-style glasses and a thick black and red-checkered flannel jacket. His jeans were worn and faded, bottomed off with a pair of brown and green camouflaged hunting boots. He had both his hands in the pockets of his bulky coat, leaning back against the wall next to the liquor store door, staring down at his boots. My first reaction was to turn and leave him be, but the dismal thought of a dry Friday got the better of me.

"Steve… Steve Campbell?" I asked, apprehensively.

101

"Hmm… wha?" He mumbled, looking up in my direction. The face I saw was one I knew—and also one I didn't. The features were the same as those I'd seen so many times in the locker room picture, but gone were the big smile and bright eyes that not even an old grainy black and white photo could hide. The face I looked at now was vacant somehow. Distant. There were wrinkles along his cheeks and around his eyes. And his eyes looked… man, his eyes looked dead.

Suddenly I wasn't so thirsty.

"What'd you say?" He asked, looking at me with those empty eyes. "You say my name, man?"

"Uh, yeah. You're Steve Campbell, right?"

He stood there, staring at me quietly. I could tell he was trying to figure out who I was. "Yeah, that's me," he said. "Who're you?"

"Oh, sorry," I replied. "I'm Mark Jansen. Janice Lewison—actually Janice McElroy now—is my stepsister. I think you guys went to school together."

He thought about that for a moment and then seemed to relax. For the first time, I could see a small smile on his face. "Oh, yeah, I remember Janice."

"She's married now, living over in Bridgecross Heights with her husband Bobby and…"

"Janice Lewison," Steve cut me off. I don't think he'd heard a word I'd said about her marriage. "Wow, man, another blast from the past tonight. Go figure." He chuckled to himself, then grew quiet again, looking back down at the ground.

"Uh… yeah," I said, even though I knew he wasn't listening.

He didn't speak.

I stood awkwardly looking at the top of his head, wondering what the heck to do next. I was starting to think that he was either drunk or high. Frustrated, I decided to give up and turned to walk away.

"How… how'd you know me?" He suddenly asked from behind me.

I stopped and turned to face him again. "Oh. I seen your picture in Coach Payton's office. You know… the all-league one from 1978. That's the year Janice graduated, so I figured you two musta known each other."

"I didn't know her too well. Kinda casual. She mostly hung out with a different crowd than me. His smile grew. "You play ball?"

"Yeah. Junior Varsity team. Wingback."

"Hey, man, I saw you play yesterday. Fast sucker! You guys looked damn good out there. How'd the varsity team do tonight? I wasn't... I didn't get to the game." The smile left his face.

"Lost, man. 35 to 27. They're not having that good a season."

His smile returned as quickly as it had vanished. "I know what you mean. Ain't been much to brag about 'round here since we won the league in '78. I can't believe Coach Payton is still around."

"You're not kidding."

It was true. Eighteen years later, and Coach Payton was still in charge of the varsity squad, despite the fact that he'd failed to win a championship since that '78 season. Two things are sacred in a small town: high school football and loyalty. That's why all-league news stories from 1978 still decorated the locker room walls in 1996, and that's why Coach Payton was still Coach Payton.

I was smiling now. I was growing more confident that I was going to get the beer I wanted after all. "You guys sure kicked some ass back then. You and Pete Martin."

Steve's smile didn't leave, but his blank eyes suddenly turned sad. "Yeah... we did."

The new look in his eyes made me worry that I might lose my chance. "Anyways... Steve. I was wondering if maybe you could buy some beer for me and my girlfriend. Um, I mean, if it's cool with you, and all. I can give you five extra bucks to buy something for yourself if you want."

He closed his eyes. "Yeah, we did," he repeated in a whisper.

"Huh?"

He shook his head. "Nothing. Hey, yeah, I'll buy for you guys. Don't gotta give me any money, but can you give me a ride home? My wife and I got in a little, uh... argument tonight, so I took a walk to blow off some steam. But, man, it's too cold to walk back. You know how it is."

I thought of Angie's hissy fit in the car and nodded. "No problem, man." I handed him twenty bucks. "We just need a twelve of Coors Light. I prefer something stronger, you know, but I got the woman with me." I cocked my thumb back toward The Boat and smiled. "You know how it is."

This time Steve nodded. "Believe me," he said, "I know."

He turned and walked into the store. I turned and walked back to The Boat.

#   #   #

"What'd he say?" Angie asked as I closed the door.

"He's gonna do it. He wants a ride home, though."

"Where's his car?"

I shrugged. "I don't know, Ang... I didn't ask. Guess he walked here and doesn't want to walk back. It's cold as hell out there." I didn't mention the fight with his wife.

"Whatever," said the Alicia Silverstone-wannabe. "God, I hope this doesn't get back to my mom."

The leftover heat from our trip to the store was nearly gone from the inside of the car, so I fired The Boat up and cranked the defroster into high. Angie remained silent as I fiddled with the radio dial. I settled on a classic rock station, keeping the volume low, as Steve climbed into the backseat with a medium-sized paper bag in hand. He handed my change to me over the seat.

"They were out of Coors Light, so I got you guys some Bud. That okay?"

"Yeah, sure," I said. "Hey, Steve, this is my girlfriend, Angie Stadler."

They shook hands and both said "Hi" at the same time.

"You care if I crack one of these open right now?" Steve asked, letting go of Angie's hand and looking at me. From the corner of my eye, I could see Angie's face tense up; she hated when other people drank in the car. I ignored her. I was anxious to get Steve home so I could start in on the remaining eleven.

104

"Go ahead, man," I said, dropping The Boat into reverse. "And thanks for helping us out." Angie crossed her arms again.

"No problem," Steve replied. "I remember what a bitch it used to be to get brewskys on a Friday night."

"Wasn't the drinking age lower then?" I asked, hoping to make small talk.

"It was eighteen then, but there weren't as many places to buy. This town used to be even smaller if you can believe it. And Coach Payton was pretty strict about his players drinking, so we always had to be careful." He lifted the beer he'd opened to his mouth and took a long swallow, then let out a small belch. "I hung out with Pete Martin, though, and you know how those quarterbacks are, always getting what they want, no matter what. He always came through with booze one way or another."

"Man," I said, looking at him in the rearview mirror as I pulled out onto the street, "you guys were pretty good friends, huh? What was it like to win a championship? Musta been the shit!"

"Yeah, we were like brothers. Hell, we're still pretty tight. Both of us work over at the Ford plant. We were supposed to go to the game together tonight, but I guess he wasn't feeling too good." He paused for a few seconds. "Oh, I forgot. I live out on Kaiser Road, just outside of town. You know how to get there?"

"Uh- huh. Old dirt road. Me and Angie have been out there a coupla times. Good place to…" Angie hit the side of my leg with her fist. "To, uh, drink." I finished.

"Yeah… right," Steve said. I couldn't see it, but I knew he was smiling. "Anyways, football was the best, man. I loved it. Best thing I ever did besides marrying my wife." I could hear him take another swig of his beer.

"How long have you been married?" Angie asked. It surprised me to hear her speak up.

"Long time… ever since after graduation. She used to go out with Pete, but he was a real popular guy then. Lotta girls after him, and I think she got sick of it. We started hanging out right after and have been together ever since. Hell, I was surprised; she was prom queen and head cheerleader and all, and I was just some dumb cornerback on the football team. I sure wasn't no flashy jock like Pete. Guess there's a lot to be said about how far a little loyalty will get you, hey?"

"Yes, there is," Angie replied. She was looking at me. About four months earlier she had found out that I'd made out with some girl at a keg party. I was stupid drunk and didn't really know what I was doing, but it still took me a couple weeks of serious butt kissing before I was able to get Angie back.

"We all stayed friends in the end, though," Steve continued. "My wife's still a looker, and I think Pete regrets to this day that he let her go." He grew silent. Faintly, the radio was broadcasting a commercial about the upcoming KISS reunion tour. "Hey, can you turn that up?" Steve asked.

"… KISS live at the Sports Arena." The deejay was saying. "Tickets go on sale at the box office on Saturday but keep tuned in here for your chance to win complimentary tickets and a limo ride to the show from KTFX, The Fox!" Immediately the first power chords of the song "Love Gun" followed.

"Kick ass tune," I said.

"Damn straight," Steve agreed from the back. "Me and Pete and his girlfriend—my wife—drove all the way to Detroit to see those guys back in '78. Best fucking show ever! I had to camp all night outside the ticket office just to get nosebleed seats, but it was worth it! It's cool to hear they're back in makeup and back together."

I was turning The Boat onto Kaiser. "How far down?" I asked.

"Third house on the right," he said. "There's probably gonna be a truck at the end of the drive, so just go ahead and park in front of the mailbox."

"Okay," I replied.

"What's your wife's name?" It was Angie again.

"Oh… uh, Mary. Used to be Mary Osterhaut. Now that I think about it, I think she used to hang out with your stepsister sometimes, Mark."

"Hm. Small world," I said, maneuvering The Boat in front of Steve's mailbox, throwing the transmission into park. His house was dark, not a light on inside or out. And there was a big red Bronco sitting at the end of the driveway, just like he'd said there'd be.

"Small town," Steve corrected. "Hey, do you mind if I finish my beer before I get out? And can you kill the lights? Don't want Mary to know I'm back yet."

"Uh, sure," I said, flicking the headlights off. Ace Frehley was breaking into one of his patented guitar solos as I did.

"You ever notice how Ace Frehley's guitar always sounds sad?" Steve asked before taking another drink. "I mean, I've always thought it was some kind of expression of how he felt about things with KISS."

I wasn't sure what he was getting at, but I listened.

"I mean," he continued, "Paul Stanley and Gene Simmons always got the credit for their success, mainly because they were the lead singers, I guess. But I still think that Ace's playing had a lot more to do with it then he ever got credit for." He took another drink.

"Yeah," I agreed, ready for him to leave so I could get my Friday night going. "He does play a mean guitar."

"But it's more than that, man," he answered. "It's like football. Pete was my friend and all, but just because he was this fancy quarterback, he got most of the notice for our championship. But us other players had a lot to do with it, you know? Used to royally piss me off that he always got what he wanted. Maybe that's why Ace left KISS for so long: to get his due." He killed the beer and crushed the can. "Sometimes you think you're doing everything right, but people still look elsewhere. It's fucked up, man." He reached for the door handle. "At least KISS found a way to fix things up. Guess there's always a way."

Trying to change the subject, I looked at the big Bronco sitting in the drive. "Nice truck," I said.

"It's not mine," he replied. I didn't ask. He continued: "Can you do me one more favor, kid? I gotta run in the house and get something real quick that I wanna give you. Shouldn't take long."

"Oh… Okay," I said, confused. "Yeah. We'll wait."

He opened the door, stepped out, then turned and looked back in, first giving Angie a strange glance, then facing me. "You always gotta be careful," he said, then shut the door.

As he opened the front door of his house and walked in, Angie looked at me. "What the heck was that all about?" she asked.

For the second time that night, I shrugged. "I have no idea. He said he was fighting with his wife. I guess it was bothering him more than he let on. I wonder what he wants to bring m…"

Suddenly there were two loud pops from inside the house. I was looking at Angie, and from behind her I could see the darkened front windows of the place light up at the same time with two quick flashes.

"What the…?" I whispered. Angie jerked her head around.

The front door of the house swung open, and Steve walked out. In one hand he held something red and white—it looked like a small blanket from where we were. His other hand was in his coat pocket.

He stepped over to my side of the car. I nervously rolled down the window.

"Here, kid." He handed me the red and white thing through the open window. It was his old football jersey. "They were cheating on me, man, cheating on me. I knew it for a while."

Then he stepped back, pulled the pistol he was hiding from his pocket, put it against his head, and fired.

Angie screamed.

I froze.

Ace Frehley's guitar was crying on the radio.

#   #   #

About a week after it happened, I met Coach Payton in his office. I wanted to give him Steve's old jersey; I didn't know what else to do with it. I handed it to him, and he just sat staring at it in his lap for a few minutes.

"You know, Mark," he finally said, not looking up from the jersey. "We won that '78 championship because of Stevie. He saved our butts in the title game against Tinsdale. In the fourth quarter they tried to run an end reverse on us, and it damn near worked, damn near fooled everybody. Except Stevie. He tackled the guy just in time to stop a touchdown, and we ended up winning that game by three points." He looked up at me with a sad smile. "I asked him after the game how he knew they were running a reverse, and he told me that he didn't at first, but then he heard the old game announcer, Frank Johnson, all excited and screaming 'Reverse! Reverse!' over the intercom system, and he thought he'd better run the other way."

He looked away from me toward the picture of Steve and Pete on the wall. I could see a tear running down his cheek.

"Yeah," he said. "Stevie had that kinda luck all right. Always in the wrong place at the right time."

Coach Payton retired the next day.

That was two years ago.

#   #   #

My junior year of football was fairly successful. We won most of our games and had high hopes for an even better senior year. But then I broke my leg in the third practice and have been sidelined ever since. I won't see varsity action ever again.

Truth be told, I don't mind all that much.

Kyle's having a great season, though, and I'm happy for him. We're not as close as we used to be, and don't hang out that often. He and Lisa broke up a while back.

"You're lucky to have Ang," he told me right after their break- up.

For some reason, hearing him say that really got to me... really bothered me. I don't know why. It just did.

Angie and I *are* still together, although it was rough going after the night with Steve. Angie took it hard, and her mom took it even harder, not allowing us to see each other for nearly four months. I think she blamed me for the loss of her daughter's innocence, for the horror she had to witness. Hell, I think she blamed me for all of it, including what Steve did. But like Steve said, there's always a way to fix things, and Angie and I are doing our best.

Two things have definitely changed, though. For one, I've never touched another beer since that night. Not one. And Angie? Well, Angie never forgets anything anymore. She wishes she could, but she can't. ♛

109

THE LONELINESS OF MONSTERS

By Scott Pearson

Carlton, Minnesota
June 1955

GINNY SORENSON HELD A DISH towel over her eyes as she finished counting out loud then, dropping the towel, added, "Ready or not, here I come!" She could hear Danny scrambling around down the hall, trying to find the best place to hide. There wasn't much to choose from in their one-story house. He'd run past the living room as soon as she'd started counting, toward their bedrooms, where he could go in the closets or under the beds. The basement and attic were off limits for hide and seek. Outside was always forbidden. And Danny's secret place was not for fun and games.

Once, a couple years ago—when he could've gone anywhere—Danny had tried to hide under the sink in the bathroom. He'd somehow gotten his arm stuck in the U of the sink trap and panicked, screaming for help. She'd had to rub lard on his arm to pull him out of there, and he'd had a dark bruise on his elbow for a week. He'd never tried that again.

Ginny gave him a little extra time, absently finishing a Pall Mall and staring out a kitchen window toward the sun dipping behind the tall pine trees that surrounded their house. The birds—chickadees, goldfinches, sparrows—were still busy around the backyard feeder. Ginny and Danny lived in farm country, their nearest neighbor a half mile away down a dirt road.

Soon the house was quiet except for Bill Haley on the radio in the living room. Maybe Danny had sneaked back in there, across from the kitchen, while she'd been looking outside. She stubbed out the cigarette.

"Okay, I'm coming now, I mean it!" Her chair squeaked on the linoleum as she stood up from the little round table in the corner of the kitchen. Ginny hurried into the hall, only glancing into the living room. Behind the couch or the drapes... she didn't think he was in there. Past the bathroom, straight into Danny's room. Not in the closet, not under the suspicious pile of dirty clothes in the corner, not under the unmade bed.

She moved into her own bedroom. Her bed was perfectly made, the bedspread hanging down nearly to the floor. She knelt down then yanked the bedspread up. Ginny flinched at the glassy eyes staring back at her, giving a sharp yelp before recognizing one of Danny's stuffed animals.

"You put Woof there on purpose!" she shouted. She thought she heard a muffled laugh, but it was gone before she was sure where it had come from. She moved to her closet, smiling, and pulled both bifold doors open at the same time. Danny wasn't there. The butterflies always flittering in her when she didn't know exactly where he was—the reason why she didn't much like hide and seek anymore, though still his favorite game—now riled into a storm in her stomach.

Ginny ran back up the hall and into the living room. "I know where you are," she said, more for herself than Danny. *I know he's here,* she added silently, trying to keep calm as she swept back the drapes from the big picture window. The sudden motion startled a gray squirrel in a birch tree in the front yard, but there was no Danny. She tripped on the edge of the braided area rug on her way across the room, barely keeping on her feet, half falling onto the couch. She peaked over the back, expecting, knowing, that he would be wedged in tight between the bottom of the couch and the baseboard. But he wasn't there.

Sinking into the couch, Ginny tried to not let despair overwhelm her as she looked toward the front door. *Did he go outside?* He understood it was forbidden, but she knew how much he missed playing in the woods around their house. A sudden deep gasp immediately rushed out of her in a sob.

"Danny, please, where are you?"

Again, a soft giggle wafted through the house. *He was inside!* Ginny jumped up off the couch and hurried into the hallway, turning into the bathroom out of desperation. The bathtub, with its translucent shower curtain, was no hiding place, so she found herself staring down at the cabinet beneath the sink, the same cabinet he'd barely fit into the last time. Bending over, she yanked the doors open.

With a happy squeal, Danny tumbled out of the cabinet, various soaps, towels, and lotions falling out along with him. "You never woulda found me if I hadn't laughed!" Then he saw the look on her face. "What's wrong, Mommy?"

Ginny sank down to the cold tile floor, glad she was wearing blue jeans not a skirt. She grabbed him tight to her chest. "I got scared when I couldn't find you."

Danny squirmed in her arms. "I just wanted to hide real good."

She eased up, holding him at arm's length, taking a long look at his uncombed dark-blond hair, without the summer-sun bleaching it used to get, his rumpled shorts and t-shirt that should have been in the dirty clothes pile. "I—I thought for a second that you'd gone outside."

Eyes wide, he said, "No, I wouldn't do that. Never."

Ginny let him go, wiping at her eyes and nose. "I just get so scared, honey. I can't lose you again." Monday would be his second birthday since he died.

"Don't cry, Mommy." He leaned forward to hug her. "I won't ever leave you. I promise."

Ginny's younger sister Samantha dropped by Sunday morning. Before losing Danny, Ginny used to go to mass with Samantha, then they'd go to one of their houses after to make cinnamon rolls for all the kids if they'd been quiet in church. When Ginny had stopped going, Samantha still came over after dropping her kids at home but had done so less frequently this spring. She hadn't been by in weeks, so it had been a bit of a scramble when Danny spotted her car pulling up the driveway.

Sitting across from Ginny at the little kitchen table, Samantha stirred sugar into her coffee, her spoon clinking loudly against the sides of the cup. "Cream?"

Ginny got up and padded across the kitchen to the Frigidaire. "Half and half." She returned to the table with the carton and sat back down. She watched Samantha pour a healthy dollop into her coffee and return to clanking the spoon around. When Ginny could no longer stand the sharp sound, she said, "Okay, what's the matter?" She took a sip of her black coffee while she waited for an answer.

Samantha stirred a couple more times for good measure, then took the spoon out and set it on a napkin. She was still looking down at it as she said, "I was talking to Nate." Their brother lived down in the Twin Cities, where he taught high school algebra. Although he was the youngest, he'd always thought he knew what was best for his sisters. After the divorce, Ginny had finally told him what she thought of his advice, and he'd rarely talked to her directly since.

Ginny leaned back in her chair. "You must have drawn the short straw."

"We're both worried, Ginny. Since losing Danny, the divorce—"

"Don't worry, I'm fine."

"I know it's hard to talk about, especially with his birthday tomorrow." Samantha raised her head and looked Ginny straight in the eyes. "But it's been a year, and you still barely leave this house."

"I don't need to, really." Ginny looked away, out the window. The hanging bird feeder swung back and forth after a blue jay took off.

"You don't need to see your friends? Your family? Ma and Pa don't even ask if you're coming for coffee anymore."

For years all the siblings had gathered back at their parents' farm in the afternoon for coffee. Back then, none of them had lived more than a couple miles from where they'd grown up. After Nate moved south, the sisters still went for coffee four or five times a week, even as they had families. They'd show up shortly after school let out, and the adults would sip their coffee while the kids had chocolate milk and then ran around in the hayfield or played in the barn or climbed trees.

She turned back toward Samantha with a sad smile. "It seems so long ago."

"We all miss you. Father Francis still asks after you. Everyone in town does."

"Tell them I'm fine."

"But you need to get out. What about a job? We sure could use an extra girl at the bank—"

"No. Martin still supports me."

Samantha put her coffee cup down hard. "When he's sober enough to hold a job."

Ginny shook her head. "He's doing better."

"Well, lately I hear he's closing down the Northeastern most nights."

"I don't want to know about that."

Samantha took a sip of her coffee. "I'll talk to my manager. He'll—"

"I said no. You're getting bad as Nate."

Samantha picked up her spoon as if to stir her coffee again, then put it down and laced her fingers together. She stared at her hands. "Nate had an idea."

"I'll bet he did."

Samantha didn't look up. "He thinks—*we* think—you should see a doctor. You know, a specialist."

Ginny stiffened in her chair. "You mean a psychiatrist. And you agree with him?"

"It's been a year. We're just worried."

"Yeah, you said that."

Samantha finally looked up again. "Not just Nate and me. Ma and Pa too. Something's gotta change."

"I've had too much change."

"They've got clinics down in the Cities. Nate thinks they could help—"

"A clinic! You wanna commit me?" Ginny forced a laugh, trying to make it a joke, but her voice had kept getting louder, she couldn't stop it, like

114

a wave piling up, about to crash on the rocks.

Samantha's eyes welled with tears. Ginny hated herself for making her sister cry, for yelling, especially when she'd had the same thoughts herself. *Am I crazy? Because Danny's back? Because I never want to leave him? Because I rush home from town with groceries, afraid he'll be gone, the house empty again?*

Samantha reached across the table and took Ginny's hands in hers. "Nothing like that. Nate says it'd just be like going in for a checkup. You'd stay with him. Sally and the girls would love to see you."

No, that wasn't possible. *If I'm not here and other people find him...* She just couldn't leave him alone, not overnight, not even one whole day. Ginny took a deep breath, letting it out as she squeezed her sister's hands.

"Thanks for worrying and trying to help. I know I should start getting out, seeing people. I'm just not up to it, not yet."

Samantha looked slightly relieved, but still a little nervous. "It's not only that. Even if—even *when*—you get out more, you'll still be living here alone. With what's going on in the world..."

Ginny frowned. "What do you mean?"

Her sister leaned closer, still holding her hands. "Maybe you haven't heard the rumors, being such a... a recluse."

"What rumors?"

Samantha stifled a shiver, as if a cold breeze had just washed over her. "People are seeing weird things. A guy was on the Duluth TV news last week, said he saw a monster."

Ginny froze for a moment, then waved a hand dismissively. "People say they see all kinds of things. Flying saucers, ghosts."

"This was close, though, just outside Cloquet, near that creepy house that—"

"I don't have a television."

"You should make Martin buy you one."

"I'll tell him you said so."

Samantha made a scoffing noise. "Yeah, he'll listen to his favorite ex-sister-in-law." She let Ginny's hands go. "I'm not kidding about the monsters.

I don't like you living alone. None of us do."

Ginny looked back out the window. "I don't feel alone."

She waited until Samantha's car disappeared around the corner of the driveway through the woods before hurrying back to Danny's room. "It's okay, you can come out now."

A small rug in the corner of the room angled up then slid off the rising floorboards. The trap door fell over on top of the rug with a soft thump as Danny climbed out of his secret place. Ginny had cut through the floorboards between the joists to make the trapdoor. In the basement beneath the trap door, within a floor-to-ceiling storage cabinet, she'd built a hidey-hole. If someone opened the cabinet, all they'd see is a clutter of camping equipment, flowerpots, and other odds and ends concealing the secret place behind the top shelves. There were pillows in the secret place, and enough room for Danny to sit up or even lie down if he curled in a ball. He kept his place well stocked with comic books, a flashlight, and his favorite cookies.

"Was that Aunt Sammy?"

"Yeah."

"I miss her and Uncle Dale and my cousins." He closed the trap door, letting it drop the last few inches. After replacing the rug, he slumped down on the floor, head hanging low.

"I know you do, sweetie."

"I wanna see them. Just them. For my birthday! They could come over, and I wouldn't go outside. Nobody else would know. Daddy wouldn't ever know."

With a sigh, Ginny smoothed out the twisted covers on Danny's bed and sat down. "It's too big a secret to ask others to keep."

"But what about surprise parties?" His last birthday party, the year before she lost him, had been a big surprise. Unbelievably, none of his cousins had spilled the beans.

"Hiding a surprise is different. A secret like this—that's just lying, and the more you lie... I can't ask them to lie for me. It's too hard. And the more who know, the easier it is for others to find out. I'm sorry."

116

"But can I still have a party?"

"Of course, sweetie, but it's just you and me."

His shoulders sagged. "I miss Louise."

Ginny turned away so he wouldn't see her frown. She didn't want to talk about Louise.

"We used to have so much fun climbing trees. She could climb so high and never got scared. 'Member when I told you about her, you thought I was pretending? 'Member?"

"Yes. Before I ever saw her. When you were always playing in the woods." That's where she'd first spotted Louise on that horrible night—eyes shining in the woods at the edge of the yard as she peered at Danny's body so small and still as he lay under the glow of the porch light, the shadows of moths fluttering across his pale face.

"She was my best friend. But she's gone now."

Ginny clenched her jaw, trying not to wonder how different everything would be if Louise had never been in the woods by their house, if Danny had never found her. Then she tried to let all that go and put a hand on Danny's shoulder to give him a gentle squeeze. He stared at the floor quietly for a couple minutes. She just watched him. They had talks like this every few weeks now. How much longer could she keep this up? How much longer could she keep everyone else at arm's length, especially after what Samantha had said? But then Danny pushed himself up off the floor and snuggled beside her on the bed, and everything else melted away, and keeping her beautiful boy close and safe was all she could think about.

Danny flopped heavily across her lap.

"Oof," she said. She only now noticed he was wearing the same dirty clothes as yesterday. "You've got other clothes, you know. You need a bath tonight."

"It was so hot in my secret place. I think I need some ice cream."

"After lunch."

"Then let's have lunch!"

"It's only ten in the morning, silly."

"But I'm *starving*!" He pulled up his striped T-shirt and sucked his belly in as far as he could. "Look, I'm caving in!"

Ginny laughed. The remaining stress from the conversation with her sister washed away as she fell back on Danny's bed, trying to catch her breath, still laughing.

Danny rolled over, pushing his face in close to hers. "What's so funny, what's so funny, what's so funny—"

"You are!" His shirt was still pulled up, so she tickled his bare belly. Danny collapsed into a pile of giggles, squirming and squealing.

Ginny just wanted their lives to be like this forever.

Ginny was combing Danny's hair after his bath when the phone rang. She stayed in the bathroom, ignoring it, thinking it could be nothing good at eight o'clock. Maybe Samantha had reported back to Nate, and her brother was finally calling her directly. Or maybe Ma was going to take her turn at convincing Ginny to get on with her life. Ginny just kept combing.

After a few more rings, Danny said, "The phone's ringing."

Smirking at him in the mirror, Ginny said, "Yes, I hear it." She finished his hair with a couple more gentle pulls of the comb, then patted him on the head. "Brush your teeth."

As she walked up the hall to the living room, she hoped whoever it was would finally hang up, but the ringing persisted. She sat down on the couch and, after waiting a last hopeful moment, picked up. There was a burst of noise before she even got the receiver to her ear. Martin, calling from the Northeastern, no doubt. She nearly hung up right away. After the morning with her sister, she really didn't want to talk with him, but if she ignored his telephone calls, he might come to the house. She could deal with that during the day, but not at night. Never again. Not when he was drunk.

"Hello," she said, raising her voice a little. She didn't want Danny to hear, but she knew Martin would hardly be able to understand her otherwise. His hearing was bad enough from working at the mill, and with the bar noise—

"Hey there, Ginny!"

She moved the receiver a couple inches away from her ear. The whole bar must have been able to hear him. "Yes, what?"

"Jus' checkin' you're okay, all alone there."

"I'm fine." She closed her eyes, wondering if he was working up to say his check was going to be late.

"I'm hearing you're maybe not so okay."

Her eyes shot open, and she felt a chill spread slowly down her body, as if she were sinking into ice water headfirst. "What?"

"Nate called. Checkin' on me, much as you, I s'pose."

Her free hand clenched tight like she'd never be able to open it again, that it would always be a knot of flesh and bone. She tried to say something, but her throat felt as clenched as her fist.

"Figure I should come over, make sure."

"No!" The word exploded from her. She lowered her voice. "No, it's late, I'm putting—" She froze; she'd almost blurted out that she was putting Danny to bed. How often had she had to say that to him before, when he'd stagger in hours late for dinner, demanding she heat something up for him? So often that it still almost came out of her mouth automatically.

"Late, it's not even nine o'clock."

"It just feels late, I'm tired. Did a lot of yardwork today."

"Yardwork." He didn't sound convinced. "I think I better—"

"I'm just going to bed early, is that okay with you and your buddy Nate?" She closed her eyes again. She was just making things worse.

"Shit, you get cranky when you're tired, just like—" He stopped. She realized she'd never heard him say Danny's name since the night they lost him, when he couldn't stop shouting it, howling it into the night sky like a wounded animal.

The silence between them seemed to engulf the noise from the bar, like there was nothing other than them, but they were packed away in separate boxes, swaddled in cloth like fragile empty bowls.

When the numbing quiet was broken by Martin's ragged intake of breath, she opened her eyes, and jumped when she saw Danny standing beside the couch, staring at her, a worried look on his face.

Danny knew not to speak when she was on the phone, but he didn't need to say anything for her to understand his fear. She forced herself to smile at him. Finally unclenching her fist, she patted him on the head, then motioned toward his bedroom. He took her hand in his and pulled. She nodded, then squeezed his hand. He let go and padded down the hallway.

"Yeah, just like," she said to Martin, and then she hung up.

Monday afternoon she'd told Danny to go play in his room while she finished getting things ready, but she heard him running down the hallway toward the kitchen when she was only half done frosting the cake. He'd been underfoot all morning while she made the cake, begging to lick the batter off the beaters after she got the pan in the oven. He wouldn't leave her be until she'd threatened to make him wash the dishes on his birthday, then he'd run from the kitchen in a blur.

"Look what I did!" Trailing behind him as he ran into the kitchen was a bunch of balloons tied together with string. When he stopped near the back door, there were still more balloons straggling behind out in the hallway.

She squinted at his accomplishment. "Is that my cooking twine?"

"What's cooking twine?"

"Never mind. Here." Finished spreading the frosting, she held out the spatula.

Danny rushed at her, free hand outstretched, the other still dragging the balloons.

Ginny raised the spatula out of his reach. "Slow down. Let go of the balloons. Then you can take this to the table."

Once he was settled at the table in the corner, sloppily licking the chocolate frosting, Ginny rinsed her hands then wiped them on her apron. She took a moment to step across the hall and look out the picture window in the living room, worried that her parents or Samantha would drop by to be with her on Danny's birthday. Part of her had wanted to postpone their little party for just that reason, but he would have been so disappointed. They were just going to have to keep a close watch.

"How many?" Danny yelled.

Coast clear, at least for now, she went back into the kitchen, a confused smile on her face. "What?"

"How many candles do I get?"

She turned away as she teared up. She knew exactly which drawer to find the candles in, the candles she'd gotten just a week before his last birthday, but which had never been used. They were right there on top, but she rummaged around in the other junk for a bit as she sniffed back more tears. Wiping at her nose with one hand, she turned around, holding the candles up in triumph in her other hand.

"How many, how many, how many?"

Ginny opened the box as she stepped over to the frosted cake. "How many did you have at your surprise party?" Sometimes he didn't remember things.

He jumped up from his seat. "Seven!"

"Right! Now come here and count out nine." She handed him the box. As he counted out his candles, she stuck them into the cake randomly.

"Can I light them?"

She took a deep breath. "Let's try one and see how it goes." He jumped around as she got the matches from a top shelf of the cupboard. "You need to settle down first, birthday boy."

Danny froze in place. He barely even moved his mouth as he said, "Like this?"

"Somewhere between being a statue and a crazy kitten." Ginny immediately regretted mentioning a kitten. They'd tried getting one after he came back, from one of the farms down the road, but the poor thing had been terrified of him. He'd cried all night when she had given it back. He was so excited now, though, he didn't seem to notice or care.

"Okay." He spoke and moved almost normally.

She held her hand over his and together they struck the wooden match. "Now be careful, but go quickly, before it burns down too far." After guiding the match to the first candle, she let go and nodded at him to continue, watching as he moved the flame briskly from wick to wick.

"Did it!" he yelled as he lit the last candle.

"Now blow it out."

He blew so hard, he put out the match and all the candles. She couldn't help it, the surprised look on his face made her burst out laughing. Danny's expression almost turned sad, but then he started giggling along with her.

When she could catch her breath, she said, "All right, let's light them again for a wish." She knew what she would wish for.

Danny had had a great birthday, first bouncing off the walls after having too much cake and ice cream, then—after settling down a little—opening the Tonka Toys dump truck she'd gotten him. He loved it. When she'd been shopping in Duluth, she'd been so nervous she would run into someone she knew who would ask who the toy was for. All that anxiety had been for no reason because she'd gotten through the shopping trip without witnesses. All through Danny's party, it had been much the same. As they played his favorite board game, Go to the Head of the Class, she'd kept glancing out the window, worrying that someone would drive up, and Danny would have to rush to his secret place while she scrambled to hide all the evidence of their celebration.

But now as she was putting him to bed, certain no one would show up this late, she could at last enjoy the moment properly, happy that the day-long party had gone uninterrupted. He'd had so much fun. Although playing Go to the Head of the Class had soured his mood for a moment as he talked about missing his friends from school, he'd bounced back when they'd made a game out of popping his balloons. He hadn't even complained when she'd said it was bedtime.

"Snuggle in, snuggle bug," she said, pulling his sheet and light blanket up to his chin. He smiled up at her, and she gave him a smooch on the forehead.

"Bedtime story?" he said.

"Always." She started flipping through some books on the shelf next to his bed.

"I miss Louise," he said.

Her sense of relief evaporated. She tried to move on. "I suppose you're too old for *Goodnight Moon* now. But I still love reading that to you. How about you pick one or two others, but we finish with—"

"Tell me what you remember about Louise. Tell me the story of how you first talked with her. That's my choice."

Ginny hated thinking about it, but oddly the story, at least the version she told, seemed to bring him some comfort—she wished she could say the same for herself—and after the other two times she'd told him, he hadn't brought up Louise for weeks. Which almost made it worth the discomfort Ginny had while telling it.

She hesitated long enough that Danny put on a pouty face and said, "It's still my birthday."

Ginny rolled her eyes at his ploy, and he looked like he was holding back laughter. "All right, *birthday boy*, but that's the last time you get to use that for a whole other year."

He just nodded his head vigorously, looking like a puppy expecting a treat. With a sigh, she leaned back against the wall and started the story.

"I was pretty lonely. Your dad moved out a month or so after you were gone. I'd almost forgotten that I'd seen Louise that night in the woods, just a glimpse, really, so fleeting that I'd almost convinced myself I'd imagined it, that she really was only your imaginary friend. I had once asked your grandma about her, though, wondering if any of the neighbors had a girl about your age staying with them over the summer. But she hadn't heard anything like that, she didn't know where a girl you met in the woods could have come from.

"I just put it out of my mind and puttered around the house every day, boxing up your clothes and toys so I could give them away to kids who needed them, but then I would just sit here on your bed, staring at the boxes all neatly labeled with their contents, carefully stacked against the wall. And instead of giving them away, I put them in your closet and closed the doors. But I never made your bed or changed the sheets or blankets, so in the morning I could come in here and lie down and pretend that you'd just gotten up and were somewhere else in the house, maybe going to the bathroom, and if I lay here long enough, you would come back and snuggle in with me."

She stopped, wiping at her eyes with the palms of her hands, trying to catch her breath so her voice would sound normal.

"Like this, Mommy?" Danny snuggled up next to her, making purring

123

sounds.

"Yes, sweetie, just like that." She pet his hair for a bit then continued. "One morning, though, as I sat here, I looked out the window, and there she was. Standing right at the edge of the yard, looking at me, but ready to run back into the woods like a scared deer. I almost couldn't believe it, like I said, I'd kind of convinced myself I'd imagined her that one time before in the dark, just a couple of eyes shining back at me.

"I blinked my own eyes, and shook my head, but she was still there. So, I motioned at her to come closer, and she did. She came right up to the house, and I opened the window, and she grabbed onto the sill and pulled herself up until her nose was pressed against the screen.

"'You must be Louise,' I said.

"'You must be Danny's mom,' she said. I thought *I should be angry, I should rage at her for drawing my boy out into the night,* but then she said, 'I miss him so much. Do you miss him? Are you lonely?'

"And in that moment, I couldn't find my rage, or my voice, only a numbness deep inside, so I just nodded. *Yes, I am lonely. So lonely.*

"Then she said, 'You don't have to be lonely. I won't ever leave you. I promise.'

"That morning was the first time I talked to her, and it was also the last time I talked to her. But she never broke her promise. And I've never been lonely since."

Ginny looked down at Danny. He was fast asleep, and she let her tears run freely.

Hours later, Ginny was still up. She was on her second bottle of Hamm's. She thought that after getting through the day and getting Danny to sleep, she'd be able to relax, but sitting alone in the living room, all the problems with Nate and Samantha came bubbling up again. Maybe the time had finally come that she just had to tell them the truth, so they'd know her odd behavior had an explanation, as unbelievable as it was. They'd see the gift she'd been given, and why she didn't want to risk losing it.

But then there was Martin. What could she do about him? She didn't want him in on this. They'd already been having trouble before they lost Danny, mostly his drinking, which had only gotten worse after—

Leafy shadows, like grasping hands, suddenly scuttled across the walls as headlights shone through the picture window. Only one person would be coming by this late. Ginny leaped to her feet at the rough sound of tires sliding on gravel and rushed out the front door after flipping on the porch light. The sense of déjà vu brought a wave of nausea as she stumbled down the steps, running across the grass between the house and the driveway, where Martin was lurching around the front of his pickup, headlights off, as he had that night just over a year ago.

He'd come home late, drunk, after the bars closed. He'd turned his headlights off as he'd come up the driveway, trying to sneak in, and hadn't seen Danny running toward the woods, hadn't known he'd hit him until he'd stumbled across his little body in front of the truck. That's when he'd started yelling Danny's name, sobbing, screaming into the moonless night. And Ginny had come running, turning on the porch light, illuminating her boy dead, her husband broken beside him. And then the eyes in the woods, Louise's eyes, suddenly knowing that she'd been real all along, that she was why Danny was outside...

Ginny, now, blinked all that away, stretching her arms out, pushing back the memories like curtains so that she could look upon what was happening here, tonight. Martin was watching her, leaning on the hood of the pickup. It was a different truck—he'd sold the old one for scrap soon after that night, unable to get behind its wheel, or even look at it.

"It's his birthday," he said, his words slurred. "Our Danny's birthday, Ginny. I'm so sorry. I can't say it enough, I can barely live with it."

She wanted to yell at him, to tell him he deserved it, but hearing him say the name, the pain reverberating in his voice, like he'd been hollowed out by grief and all that hurt echoing within him for the past year, she just looked back at him as tears again streamed down her face. He'd lived with that ache all this time, while she'd had Danny here, with her, all to herself.

Taking a step forward, closer to Martin, she said, "It's okay. We can get better, both of us."

He looked like he wanted to believe her, and the pain on his face softened. But then his gaze, slightly unfocused already, moved beyond her, and his brow furrowed. "Who's that?"

Ginny's blood seemed to chill and thicken in her veins, making her body stiff and sluggish as she turned to see what he was looking at. Her whole world tipped upside down at the sight of Louise, still in Danny's pajamas, walking toward them. Ginny opened her mouth to say something, anything, to try to explain, to stop everything from spiraling out of control, but no words emerged, just an inarticulate gasp. The moment stretched out forever, the only sound the nightly chorus of crickets and frogs in the woods. She'd never thought she'd see Louise again.

"Who—?" Martin said again, taking an unsteady step away from his truck. His drunken face focused for the first time since he'd stepped onto the driveway. "Those are Danny's favorite pajamas. What the hell?"

Ginny found her voice. "That's Louise. She's... she's visiting."

Martin turned to Ginny so quickly that it made him stagger. "What? She was pretend. You told me she was pretend."

"Martin, listen—"

"No! I don't—how long has she been here? She..." He clenched his hands into fists, then pressed them against the sides of his head, closing his eyes. "I remember, you thought Danny might have gone outside to play with Louise."

Ginny didn't remember having told him that. That night and the weeks after were a blur, as she'd practically erased the sight of Louise from her mind, telling herself she was seeing things, not wanting to wonder if she'd believed Danny, if she'd told him to have Louise over to play, if then he wouldn't have sneaked out in the night...

Martin's eyes snapped open, and he stepped toward Louise, who had come to a stop a few feet away, still on the grass. He thrust a finger at her. "Her fault? All this time..." He was getting louder, his tone turning from despair to rage. He glanced back at Ginny. "And dressed in Danny's pajamas! How could you?"

"He was my best friend!" Louise shouted, her voice holding an authority and resonance beyond her little-girl frame, as if she'd commanded Ginny and Martin to face her. "My *only* friend! *You* took him away from us. Left Mommy *and* me alone. You don't belong here, it's just us now."

Martin took a step back from the imposing child, reaching a hand toward Ginny for support. "I don't understand..."

Ginny wanted to explain, to repeat what Louise had told her that morning at the window, that being there when Danny died, she—it—had absorbed many of his thoughts and memories, that it could be Danny as easily as Louise, that it would be even easier, more comfortable, to become Danny, because it had made up Louise while fleeing some other people, hadn't remembered having a name before Danny had found it alone and lost in the woods. Danny had named her, helped her feel safe. But before Ginny could try to find the right words, Martin's face went pale and slack as Louise became Danny.

Martin fell to his knees. "My boy, my—"

But then it was Louise again, a hard look on her face.

Martin scrambled backward, getting uneasily to his feet, sobbing in confusion.

Ginny reached out for the child. "Louise—Danny—please stop." But Louise continued advancing on Martin as he retreated toward his pickup, taking uneven steps backward, never taking his eyes off the angry girl.

"We don't need you. We don't need anyone," Louise said, but the voice was Danny's, and it made Martin stop in his tracks. "Get out of here, leave us alone."

Martin wiped his arm across his face, took a deep breath, released it, and steadied his stance. "No, I'm not leaving my boy again. Not until I understand—"

Louise exploded forward in a reshaping blur of writhing tentacles and chitinous claws, flailing, grasping, as Ginny screamed and lunged for the mismatched creature, getting a grip on something, some sort of feeler or eye stalk, digging her heels into the gravel. She didn't think it touched Martin, but he tumbled over backward hard. His head hit the bumper of his truck with a sick thud, underscored by a wet cracking sound in his neck.

Ginny fell on her side in the driveway, gravel scratching across her face and bare arms. Whatever she'd had hold of slipped from her fingers, skittering and clattering away, leaving her palms cold and slimy. She didn't move, just stared at Martin, also unmoving.

She went numb all over. Were her eyes even blinking? Everything in her life was broken, with no way to fix it. She wondered if she could just lie here until Samantha found her, found them, no matter how many days that might be. Then Nate could come and take her away to the Cities, where she could try to make sense of the last year of her life, and maybe they would know something about these monsters. But what about Danny, where was he now?

Behind her she heard the door of the house open and close. Heavy footsteps across the porch, then muffled upon the grass, until finally the crunch of gravel circled around her and a pair of Martin's old work boots from the basement entered her view, stopping a yard away.

She twisted her neck, felt sand sticking to blood on her cheek. Craning to look up, she saw Martin standing over her in musty, wrinkled clothes. Shifting her eyes, she also saw his body lying still in front of the pickup, the shadows of moths fluttering across his pale face.

The Martin looming above her said, "We don't have to be lonely. I won't ever leave you. I promise." ♜

EXPIRATION DATE

By Steven Philip Jones

"CAN THE LIVING HAUNT THE dead?"

Brad Chambers turned away from the refrigerator. "What did you ask?"

Aldin Norton repeated his question.

"Is that some kind of Zen riddle?" Chambers rummaged until he found a jar of mayonnaise. Twisting off the cap, he walked to the kitchen's island, where other sandwich makings waited. "When a guy forgets to eat lunch, his brain isn't up to penetrating conundrums."

"No riddle. Call it a flight of fancy."

"Fancy requires an imagination, Al, and you don't have one. Maybe I'm missing one, too, since I don't have a clue what to tell you." Sniffing the mayonnaise, Chambers wrinkled his nose. "*Phew!*"

"Has it soured?"

"Smells like." Chambers searched the jar for an expiration date. "Yes," he frowned, then paled. "Oh."

"What?"

"Nothing." Chambers blushed.

Norton stood away from the counter he was leaning against, reached across the island and confiscated the jar. Reading the date, he sneered. "It's just a coincidence, Brad."

"Sure. Still, though…"

"It's the day Connie died. I understand." Norton screwed the lid on and tossed the mayonnaise into a trashcan. "I suppose an inventory of my refrigerator is overdue. I should have remembered to do that."

"She's only been gone three months."

"What does that mean?"

"You're still adjusting to life without her. I'm sure she used to take care of stuff like that."

Norton had no idea. He imagined Connie did. Norton remembered that during their first few years of marriage he almost always found her in the kitchen when he came home from work. Even when the hour was well past midnight, Connie would be here, waiting up for him. "Do you want some dinner?" Usually, he would tell her he needed to get some sleep for the following day, and gradually Norton came home to find Connie already in bed. That was on the nights Norton managed to make it home, of course.

He raised and lowered his shoulders. "If you want to get morbid about dates, Brad, today would have been my and Connie's nineteenth wedding anniversary."

"It is?" Chambers remembered it was. "Sorry, Al. I forgot."

"This is getting me off the point. I asked you over because I want to talk about my will. I need to make an addition."

"Sure thing." Chambers shuffled the makings into a sandwich, took a bite, and swallowed. "Name it."

"I want something interred with me in my coffin when I die."

"Like what? A Bible? You get religion?" Chambers took another bite, but forgot to chew when Norton, an earnest man even when his company's stock split, chuckled. "I say something funny?"

"In a way. Never mind. I want a codicil entered into my will instructing that an antique bottle be placed in my coffin with me."

Several questions came to Chambers' mind. He started with: "What bottle?"

"Just a bottle. Not very large."

"Why do you want to be buried with it?"

"My motive is irrelevant. Can you arrange it?"

Chambers had to think about that. Hadn't he heard about people being buried with their favorite set of golf clubs or inside their Cadillac? "I guess. If that's what you want."

"I do."

"All right. I'll see what I can do. Where's the bottle?"

Norton appeared chary. "Why?

"I imagine it should be described in your will, probably by an appraiser. And I suppose I ought to leave instructions where you keep it for when your time comes."

"Oh. Yes. That makes sense. I don't have it here. I'll bring it by your office tomorrow. After that, I'll keep it on the nightstand in my and Connie's bedroom."

"All right." Norton laid his sandwich down. Talking about coffins and wills had put him off his appetite.

#   #   #

Norton brushed his black forelocks out of his face and squinted his gray eyes against the setting sun as he approached the antique shop. *Atticus's Curiosities and Mysteries*. He still thought the name sounded like something from one of the Ray Bradbury stories he had read as a kid. "Back when I had an imagination," he muttered as he opened the door.

Inside, the shop was musty from moldering antiques, poorly lit, and, as had been the case during Norton's earlier visits, vacant of other customers. He wondered how the crooked little old-timer who owned the business managed to pay the bills. The proprietor was friendly enough, Norton supposed, and had already wrapped Norton's order, so at least the codger understood how to treat customers. The shop's location could have been better situated, although today it worked to Norton's benefit, being quite close to the burial ground.

As sunlight faded to gloaming, Norton walked through the graveyard's filigreed arched gate and followed a rutted brick carriage road to his wife's grave. After Connie's melanoma was diagnosed, she had instructed her husband and Chambers that she was to be laid to rest in her family's ancestral plot. "It's a tradition," she told them. Since the 17th century the Weatherbys had been buried beneath a capacious willow in the burial ground's eldest section. His wife had come from old blood.

Norton was new rich. (He refused to use that silly French phrase.) The independent grandson of an immigrant named Khrennikov, he grew up breathing the soot of a Westmoreland County, Pennsylvania coal mine. Working his way through college and an Ivy League MBA, Norton then parlayed everything he had learned into building Nome America, a high-tech corporation whose assets could have allowed him to retire when he was 35. It wasn't in him to slow down, though, even after Connie began growing more and more distant during the long hours Norton dedicated to his business. In hindsight, he wasn't surprised. Connie had never worked for her money. How could she understand why he was compelled to work for his? Despite this distance, however, it had crushed Norton when Connie insisted on being buried with her family, instead of in the mausoleum he had had built for him and her near the burial ground's front gate.

"Not for me," she had told him. "And not with you."

If the cancer hadn't already been saving him the bother, Norton might have killed Connie right then.

Splitting the willow's curtain of narrow leaves with one hand, he passed through to the shady idyll beneath the tree's umbrella. The failing daylight sifted through the catkins, creating patterns of interlacing lines as if it was shining through a tracery, while the earth and grass seemed as pungent as the odor from an ancient Egyptian embalmer's shop.

"Happy anniversary, dear."

Norton stopped on Connie's grave without looking at her stone. Unwrapping his purchase, he removed a lapis bottle, about the size of a large dagger, and dropped Atticus's paper on the ground.

"Not up yet, I see. I've brought you a present."

Removing a stopper, Norton placed the bottle neck-down on top of Connie's stone.

"I'm afraid I'll have to take it back in the morning." He tucked the stopper into a pants pocket. "Brad has to see it. After all, the man was your lapdog. Fortunately for me he's a lawyer and sells his services to anyone who can afford his retainer."

Norton thought about what he just said.

"'Retainer'? Now *that* is ironic."

Norton chuckled then whistled as he left the Weatherby plot then the burial ground, a gibbous moon rising as he walked through the arch.

#   #   #

"What's so special about this?" Chambers turned the bottle over in his big hands. "What's it made out of?"

Norton told the lawyer it was lapis lazuli. When Chambers asked what that was: "A semi-precious stone. One ancient civilizations were very fond of. As early as the fourth millennium B.C. the city of Ur had a thriving trade in lapis, and it's frequently mentioned in the Bible. The columns of St. Issac's Cathedral in Petersburg are lined with lapis."

"Sounds like you did get religion."

"I thought I'd told you that my grandfather was Catholic. Anyway, people in the Middle Ages believed lapis lazuli could free the soul of fear and envy."

"Wouldn't that be nice? What's with all these symbols carved on it? They Greek?"

"No. Those are cuneiforms. But it does have a Greek name. It's called an *eusplanknos* jar."

"What's an *eusplanknos* jar?"

"The word means 'strong-bowelled.'"

"That sounds sort of gross." Chambers took a closer look at the stopper. "Anything in here?" He grabbed the stopper. A college defensive back who still benched twice his own weight, Chambers grunted as he tugged then pulled without success. "Man!"

"The stopper and jar are actually one piece carved out of a single stone."

133

"Looks like it should pull out." Chambers quit trying. "It's all one piece? Then it's not really a jar, is it?"

"It's a memento from a second honeymoon Connie and I took a couple of years after we were married. Whenever I hold it, I feel very close to her. That's why I want it interred with me."

"Oh." Chambers placed the bottle on his desk. "Yes. I guess that was a rough deal for you."

"I forgot until the other day that Connie had put the bottle in storage. That's why I couldn't give it to you yesterday. I had to go fetch it."

The lawyer's eyebrows went up. "I didn't know Connie had anything more left in storage."

Norton almost kicked himself for getting too clever. "Well, you may be our lawyer, but you don't know everything about our estate. Connie and I had some knick-knacks stored away before we moved into where we… where I live now."

"'Knick-knacks'?" Chamber cocked his head. "Whatever. I can take it to the appraiser this morning and have him write up that description for your will."

"Fine, so long as I can have the bottle back today."

"Well, if you want to pay extra, I suppose the appraiser should be able to finish by five."

"Do it."

"All right." Chambers stared at the bottle again and wondered why Norton was lying to him.

#   #   #

"I don't know, doc. I just have a bad feeling about it."

Dr. Tamar Hasan, a friend of Chambers' father and professor of archaeology, listened to the lawyer as he scrutinized the bottle under a fluorescent magnifying glass. "It doesn't appear to be anything extraordinary. Although I've never seen a bottle quite like it before." He touched the stopper. "You say it's one piece?"

"That's what my client said. I think that's a lie."

Hasan put the jar next to his right ear and tapped the sides. "Difficult to tell, but an MRI should show us if it's at least hollow or not. Even if it is, why should you suspect there is anything sinister about this bottle?"

"I can't go into details about that. Attorney-client privilege. All I can say is that I know more about this client's estate than the person would like me to know."

That sounded like something more than professional courtesy to Hasan. "Let's just say that then. Your client called this an *eusplanknos* jar?"

"Yes."

"Are you sure?"

"Positive. He said it was Greek for `strong-bowelled'."

"Well, Roman, actually. The Greek word *eusplanknos* has a different connotation. Nonetheless, I've never heard of a jar with such a name."

"Do those cuneiforms tell you anything?"

"Not really. They're Sumerian. The ones I recognize are anyway. There are quite a few I don't recall ever seeing before. Undoubtedly this is an ancient bottle. Very ancient. One I wouldn't mind borrowing for study."

Chambers shook his head. "I told my client he'd have it back by the end of the business day."

"Unfortunate." Hasan's lower lip pouted. "Fortunately, the MRI will not take long, leaving enough time to photograph it and make some rubbings. Perhaps take some clay impressions. None of that will be as convenient as having the actual artifact on hand but should provide me with adequate research material. Once I find out anything, I'll let you know."

"Thanks, doc." Chambers thought about Connie, alive and laughing and full of spirit. Beautiful. "Call me as soon as you do."

#   #   #

Driving out to the Nome technology campus, Chambers was shown into Norton's office, although "suite" seemed a more appropriate noun to Chambers. Norton's office had its own bathroom, gym, sauna, even a dental

135

chair so the boss could have his teeth drilled without missing any time from work. And there was a private bedroom, but Chambers, having been Connie's friend, didn't like to think about that place.

"Can I get my nickel deposit?" the lawyer cracked as he returned the bottle. Norton examined it, not for chips or cracks, Chambers sensed, but tampering. "Anything wrong?"

"Doesn't appear to be. Did your appraiser finish?"

"Sure did. I'll file the papers tomorrow and then you and your trusty companion will be good to go."

Norton stood the bottle on his desk. "Fine. You'll never know what all this means to me."

"Just earning my pay, Al. Anything else?"

There was, but nothing Chambers expected.

"You loved my wife, didn't you?" Norton's tone was more statement than query.

"Pardon me?"

"You loved Connie. One of those platonic from-a-distance passions I would have expected from a troll devoid of social skills. Why else would you still be the lawyer for our estate? You can't stand me."

"We've been friends since our freshman year! Before you met Connie!"

"We were different people then, and you don't like the person I've become. Neither did Connie."

Not sure what to do with his hands, Chambers stuffed them into his pants pockets. "Why are you asking this?"

"You're not denying it?"

"I have no intention of dignifying it!"

"That's what people with morals say when they don't want to lie. You're a lawyer, Brad. You sold your morals when you passed the bar."

A notion of what Chambers could do with his hands popped into his head, but the thought of being arrested for assault didn't appeal to him.

"Al, Connie was one of the most decent persons I knew. You weren't half bad yourself until a few years ago. And I doubt I'm telling you something you don't already know, but almost every guy who met your wife had a crush on her. She was that kind of woman."

Norton slid his eyes to the bottle. "Is that an admission of guilt, counselor?"

"Take it as one, if you want. While you're at it, you might as well know that I think you're an A-plus jackass for ignoring Connie the way you did, especially at the end. Just to build your empire here. And for what? Maybe to leave something behind when you and that whatever-it-is jar are filed away in your crypt? To achieve some sort of immortality? That's what family is for, Al. That's what Connie could have given you. Wanted to give you."

"Nothing lasts forever, Brad. Not even family. Everything spoils with time, especially marriages. Maybe you have to have been in one to know that."

"Believe that malarkey if it lets you sleep at night. The truth is that the real deal was there for the taking and you..." Chambers followed Norton's eyes. "You threw it away like a note in a bottle."

Norton barked laughter.

"What is wrong with you?"

Norton waved a hand—as if to say, "You wouldn't believe me!" —and collapsed into his desk chair.

"Maybe I had a thing for Connie, pal, but you're the one going nuts now that she's gone." Chambers turned and got out of the office, trembling, afraid of what he wanted to do to Connie's husband.

Behind him, Norton continued laughing.

#   #   #

Getting home late, Norton put the *eusplanknos* jar on the nightstand then sat on the bed to stare at his prize.

"That was some scene at the office, eh?" he said to the bottle. "If only Brad knew how much I'd been looking forward to it. If he only knew..."

Knew how right he was, his thoughts interrupted.

Grinding his palms into his tired eyes, Norton lay down, trying to block out the memory of how the loneliness of his empty house had irritated him after Connie's funeral. How it had grated on him until, one night, he went to the burial ground just to be near his dead wife.

If only I did that sooner.

Norton stared at the bottle until he fell asleep. And then he dreamed.

Dreamed he walked unafraid in the dark down the burial ground's rutted brick road. Dreamed he cursed the moon as it hid behind a cloud and at a mid-summer's ground haze that made it impossible to see his feet.

Norton grumbled until he found the willow then stumbled until he reached the tree and stepped through its canopy.

The mist, thicker here, obliterated all of the markers.

In the sky the moon tossed away the cloud and lanced the willow's crown with a silver shaft of light.

The diameter of the moonbeam widened until it illuminated everything beneath the tree, never mind the leaves, and condensed the fog, creating pockets of eddies.

The swirling gave Norton vertigo.

Nauseous, he lurched towards the willow's trunk.

Grabbing tight, like a sailor clinging to a mast during a storm, he watched sparks ignite within the mist, dim and buoyant as fireflies, then bright as flash paper and wild as dryads.

Then Norton heard a laugh, and his spine shook his ribs.

It was Connie's laugh.

He jerked awake. Sat and snatched up the bottle to make sure it was real. Relieved that it was, Norton almost smiled.

\#   \#   \#

Time passed. Norton fired Chambers, and Chambers made it a point to visit Connie's grave at least once a week. He brought flowers on holidays and important personal dates, weeded when necessary, brushed away dead leaves in the fall, cleaned her stone with Windex after the harsh winter, and talked. As far as he could tell, Norton never came here to pay his respects.

\#   \#   \#

The Nortons' twentieth wedding anniversary was less than a week away when Hasan called Chambers to ask the lawyer to come to the university and meet a colleague.

"This is Professor Mary Considine. We've known each other since graduate school." Hasan's colleague was the physical antithesis of the doctor. Tan and fit, Considine looked to be closer in age to Chambers' 42 than Hasan's 58. "She's been in Kuwait the past few years, excavating a fascinating ziggurat. It appears to have been part of a temple compound for a city built by a sect that broke away from Sumer sometime around 3400 B.C.E."

Considine spoke with a Northeastern New England accent and demonstrated an impressive grip as she shook Chambers' hand and wasted no time asking if she could see the *eusplanknos* jar. "I've seen shards, but nothing close to an intact artifact. Judging by the epigraphy in the impressions Tamar made from it, I'd have to say this particular bottle is at least fifty-three hundred years old. Marvelous!"

Chambers hated telling the enthusiastic woman, "No. I'm afraid I've parted ways with the client who owns the bottle. Under less than pleasant circumstances."

"Sounds personal," Considine commented.

"It was. I doubt my former client would even accept a phone call from me now. Listen, the doc here couldn't tell me much about the bottle the last time we talked. Just that the MRI showed it was hollow and it may have something inside it."

"Yes, he showed me. My guess is it contains a human heart."

"What?"

"As best as we can tell, the purpose of an *eusplanknos* jar was to provide the soul of a deceased person with a place of solitude to meditate or, if need be, suffer prolonged isolation before it could pass into the Afterlife. These Sumerians called this period 'gestation,' a term that I believe contemporary Egyptians borrowed to give a name to their own belief in a period preceding the rebirth of the soul. I also suspect some of these jars eventually found their way to Rome, where the cuneiforms for 'gestation' were mistaken for 'digestion,' leading to the erroneous name *eusplanknos* or 'strong-bowelled' jar.'"

"Or," suggested Hasan, getting caught up in his friend's train of thought, "considering what was put into these jars, *eusplanknos* here could be the Greek adjective 'tender-hearted,' as it is used in Ephesians 4:32."

Chambers: "These Sumerians you're studying stuffed people's hearts in these bottles?"

Considine: "Actually they sliced the hearts so they would fit through the neck." She picked up one of the clay impressions of the lapis bottle and pointed to the cuneiforms Hasan had not recognized. "These pictographs, as far as anyone knows, are unique to this sect. Their purpose appears to have been to compel the soul to enter the jar, hold it inside once the jar was sealed, and repel any malicious spirits that may try to free the soul inside and prevent justification."

"What's that?"

"'Justification?' The process by which a soul is judged so it may enter the Afterlife. If you watch the Discovery Channel you may know that ancient Egyptians believed Osiris, god of the Afterlife, weighed the heart of a deceased person on a scale, and, if the scale tipped towards truth and justice, the deceased's soul was allowed to enter. From what I've been able to decipher, it appears this Sumerian sect believed that their god Enki performed much the same ritual. They also believed that without gestation, justification would be impossible for any but the pure-hearted."

"So, what if a heart tipped the scale the other way?"

"The Egyptians believed that the deceased's soul was devoured by a monster."

"That's harsh."

"On the other hand, this Sumerian sect seemed to believe that the deceased's soul would be barred from the Afterlife and become something akin to what the Egyptians called tutelary spirits."

"That doesn't sound so bad."

"Egyptian tutelary spirits were demons who could be either kind or vengeful, but apparently this Sumerian sect believed tutelary spirits were always the latter since they could never pass into the Afterlife. This made them spirits that humans were better off avoiding."

"Sounds sort of cruel."

"So is storing a person's heart in a jar. The concept of putting a soul in a bottle was symbolic, like the Eucharist's bread and wine. In this instance, a deceased person's heart is removed, carved, and then stored in one of these jars to represent the soul."

Chambers almost gagged and not entirely from this image. He could hear Norton telling him, *"Whenever I hold it, I feel very close to her."*

"Professor Considine, I need you to tell me one more thing about this bottle."

#   #   #

Norton, as usual, was late getting home.

Parking in the garage, he waited for the automatic door to shut before he got out of his Lexus and entered his house through the connecting door.

Turning lights on and off as needed, he proceeded upstairs to the bedroom.

Turning on the bedroom light, he shouted.

Chambers was sitting on his bed, back propped against the headboard, holding the *eusplanknos* jar.

"What do you think—?"

"Shut up, Al." Chambers' voice was quiet and calm enough to intimidate Norton.

"How'd you get in here?"

Chambers held up a key.

"You and Connie—?"

"Were just friends, but there were lots of nights you weren't here that she needed to talk."

For some reason Norton would have preferred hearing that the two had been having an affair. In some ways, perhaps they had.

"Al, what's in this bottle?"

"Nothing. I told you, it's carved from a single piece of lapis lazuli."

Chambers told Norton about Hasan taking an MRI of the bottle and

141

then what Considine had said about *eusplanknos* jars. "Now what did you do to Connie?"

Norton said nothing.

Wrapping a hand around the bottle's stopper, Chambers tugged. "It really looks like it should pull out, even though it doesn't." Twisting hard to the right, he unscrewed the snug stopper the way Considine had instructed.

"Don't do that!"

The stopper came free. Chambers tipped the bottle over. Nothing fell out, so he shook it. Not so much as a rattle. Removing a penlight from a pocket, Chambers peaked down through the neck. "Empty." He looked at Norton. "Why'd you get so bent out of shape, Al?"

"You're damaging it. It's priceless. Give it back before I call the police."

"Go ahead. I came here expecting that one of us would call them."

"Why? Did you imagine I mutilated my wife and stuffed her heart into that bottle?"

"Why not? You cut her heart up plenty of times when she was alive. You've never been a guy who went in for knick-knacks. So why did you dish out what must have been a chunk of dough to buy an *eusplanknos* jar?"

"Why shouldn't I? Do you really think I resented Connie so much? Just because she wanted to be buried with her family rather than her husband?"

"Appears we're on the same wavelength here, Al."

"You're insane. Now put that stopper back in place and give me back my property or I will call the police."

"I'm crazy? Didn't I say you were the one going nuts now that Connie is gone?" Chambers swung his legs around to sit on the edge of the bed and stared at the bottle's strange writing. "Maybe you got it into your head that this thing really works. Maybe you think her soul is trapped inside here. Maybe that's why you feel so close to Connie whenever you hold it." He looked up at Norton. "Do you? Are you trying to haunt Connie by putting her in this bottle?"

"That would require a vivid imagination," Norton chuckled. "Something I don't have. Remember?"

Chambers nodded. Stood. Scowled and flung the bottle near

Norton's head.

Norton ducked and heard the bottle shatter behind him.

"No!"

Chambers stomped towards Norton then past the man. "I'll be at home waiting for the cops."

Norton gawked at the brilliant blue shards on the floor behind him. Jerked his eyes in every direction but saw nothing. Outraged, he roared, "You won't have to wait long!"

Picking up the receiver from the phone on the nightstand, he dialed "9" then wailed as his chest blasted with pain.

Chambers held up at the top of the stairs and ran back to the bedroom. He found Norton standing by the nightstand, arms dangling, the receiver in his right hand.

"Al?"

No reply.

"Al!"

Norton looked over his shoulder and did something he never did. He smiled.

"What's wrong with you, Al?"

"You've always been a good friend, Brad." It was Norton's voice, of course, but there was something different yet familiar about it.

Chambers asked, "Al?", then noticed something out of the corner of one eye that almost made him yell. "Uh…are you all right?"

"I will be. Soon. But you need to go."

"You hollered like somebody had set you on fire."

For a second Norton's eyes glittered with a cruel light. "Nothing like that. Now, please, go. And don't worry."

The big man nodded. Forced himself to leave the bedroom. "You take care," he heard himself say as he stepped into the hall, then behind him heard, "You, too."

#   #   #

A few days later the police finally knocked on Chambers' door. Not to arrest him. They were searching for Aldin Norton, who apparently walked out of his house a few nights earlier and hadn't been seen since.

The police interrogated Chambers about the last time he saw Norton, and the lawyer answered their questions truthfully, except when he deleted information he was positive the police would never believe. After all, how would it help their investigation if he told the police about his breaking the *eusplanknos* jar? If he did that then he would have to tell them that he saw the bottle intact a few seconds later, capped with a stopper Chambers had no doubts he had still been clutching when he heard Norton wail.

#   #   #

"Aldin? Wake up, Aldin."

Norton opened his eyes. Or thought he did. Everything was dark. He started to panic when he realized he had no idea where he was. The last thing he remembered was…

"Connie?"

"I'm here, Aldin. Don't you feel close to me?"

Norton jerked, tried to stand up, and hit his forehead against something hard. Something else that had been lying on his chest rolled off, and he heard stone clunk against stone. He fumbled without thinking until he found the object and picked it up. Even unable to see, he realized it was the *eusplanknos* jar.

"Careful, Aldin. You might break it." Connie laughed, harsh and cruel.

"Where am I?" Norton felt around and found walls that were very close beside and above him.

"Right where you wanted us to be."

"What?"

"You left me in that bottle for about a year, Aldin, but I don't think you'll last as long in here."

"Where am I?"

"Because I can tell you, from experience, that the problem with bottling up anything too long is that eventually, one way or the other, it goes bad."

"Connie!"

"I can't help wondering when your expiration date will be, Aldin."

Connie laughed. Her husband screamed. But the Norton mausoleum had thick marble walls so even a person standing right outside the crypt would never hear them. It would be different if that person happened to step inside, but no one had any reason much less desire to do that. Not even Chambers, who drove past the mausoleum each week on his way to the Weatherby plot to visit Connie's grave. ♜

THE WHARF

By Mike Owsley

I WILL NEVER FORGET THE wharf. In moments when I was lost, in need of inspiration and in doubt that I would find any, I went to the wharf. I would sit there, quietly and in contemplation, and watch sailboats pull to safe harbor. It was always calming to me; beautiful, serene, and scenic in spite of the frigid air. I would sit there, in that place where the city met the sea, and write poem after poem of the heavy waves and rancid reek of fresh fish.

The deep, French blue waves lapped at the boardwalk around my wharf, where the sound of crying gulls punctuated the gently flapping canvas, rolled tight on the docked ships. They were each a beautiful, pearled white, with names like *Ambassador* or *Richmond*. Despite their stature, how confident they loomed, they were nothing more than ornaments on the larger wharf. They bobbed, gently, in simple fashion. The ships rocked, silently screaming their prominent inclusion in the environment.

When I met her, it seemed to be only a natural extension of the great breadth that place took on my life. I, of course, had known the wharf longer than she claimed. That source of contention, however, did not matter to me nearly as much as the woman before me did. She was, after all, the only thing able to absorb more of my thoughts than the wharf.

She invited me to her apartment, which she said overlooked the wharf. The property itself was fine, and in short order I moved in. It was a small, one bedroom affair. Plants grew in vibrant greens wherever a surface flat enough to hold one stood. Her bed was soft, inviting. I found my sleep there returned to me dreams about the wharf that had propagated in the years before I came upon the place.

I found my home immediately in this place. My walk from the wharf to that new home was an easy addition to my new routine. I would ignore the cries, the calls of the city, and enter that apartment instead. I was always greeted from my time at the wharf with cod, or bass, or some other fish filleted to my liking. The cold breeze off the Massachusetts Bay ruffled papers I'd left on the coffee table. And as music from our record player rocked us to sleep, she painted for a small art shop I knew she managed in some corner of town that was foreign to me.

In the whole of that admittedly unimpressive apartment, which often smelt like roasted coffee and freshly cooked eggs, the thing that stood out the most was her easel. She had placed it next to the window in the living room overlooking the wharf, and on it was a near completely perfect rendition of the place. Nearly perfect, that is, save for a small island with a large lighthouse on it placed carefully in the far-right corner.

When I asked her about her inclusion of a lighthouse in an otherwise masterful capturing of the wharf, she looked confused. I pointed out the missing lighthouse, and she ignored me. She told me that she always painted the wharf perfectly. I nodded, there would be no use in arguing when she had determined the meaning of her art.

The next day when we awoke, while I was preparing breakfast, I looked out the window. My mind was destroyed to discover that in the far corner of my perfect wharf, right where she had painted it, was a lighthouse. I grabbed my shoes, my pen and journal, and rushed to my usual bench.

While there, I wrote about this new world. The lighthouse seemed to be turned off, unmanned. I do not ever remember seeing it, a feeling that twisted and burned in shame and confusion. I flipped through my pages, desperately and depraved, until I found the source of the question in my mind. It was a poem, with a simple title, *Lighthouse*, and a description perfectly matching what I saw before me. The tall, white tower that came to a point was described in poetic prose in frantic scribbles, written months ago.

It was at that moment that I realized there was something about the wharf I would never be able to understand. My brain was wracked with each desperate attempt to remember the lighthouse, or the rock covered island that made its berth on. My wharf seemed fuller, more alive, but its core was disturbed.

When I opened my poetry book, I found that any verse that poured from my mind had to include the lighthouse. Its stalwart defense of the wharf made it an impossibly permanent feature. I didn't understand how I could forget the existence of the lighthouse. How could one of the single most important parts of the wharf become lost in my mind?

With each passing day, I regarded the abandoned lighthouse with the revelry it deserved. There was a strange peace amongst the wharf, a peace that I was sure was provided by the ever-present lighthouse. I began to write about the people who I imagined had once inhabited the lighthouse. Whatever defenders had guarded the wharf and its tranquil living had clearly done a supernaturally effective job. I wrote in length about the thing that lurked beneath the sea, what I called the Beast in the Bay.

I found that new chapters would come to me in wild fits. I would not touch the damn thing for weeks, but then I would awake in the middle of the night with a new part to the story. I would write thousands of words in hours, and then nothing would come to me until my next fever. In those times, I came to move around the wharf more than I had in the past. I migrated away from my bench, my humble perch since graduate school, to map each and every single unfound nook of the wharf. It was there I learned the smell of the fish market, far down the wharf and stocked with new catch from the day, and the taste of sea spray soft on my face.

Despite sending it to a small publication, I found myself inexplicably popular with my story of the wharf. I had begun to receive letters in the mail, my supporters told me how once they read my book, they could not stop thinking about the wharf themselves. In hurried correspondence I regarded their feelings and shared my own. Their dreams were eerily similar to mine, and they thanked me for freeing their memories. All I was prideful I had shown them such a great world, but hesitant to share the knowledge of my wharf.

During this time my relationship thrived on abundant love. I think fondly of borrowing a pleasure ship, a white sailboat that a friend of hers loaned her. We never left the dock, neither of us found a need to leave the safety of the wharf. There we would laugh, talk, love, eat. While it was the source of both of our inspiration, the way we had come to find each other, the wharf seemed to melt away around her raucous giggle and eyes as French blue as the bay around us.

When she revealed her next painting to me, it was after my first novel had been published. There it was, again, the same perfected painting depicting the living and breathing wharf. Only, I noticed, that this depiction of the wharf included, inexplicably, a great hand reaching out of the darkness of the sea to clasp the surface. It was carved, scaled, and godly, a mighty hand with a raw strength that steeled my very soul.

She again mentioned that the wharf had, in her eyes, always included a hand so great it could hold the state of Rhode Island in its palm. As surely as she believed it, I looked into the pages of my novel, and the letters I had been sent. Many messages concerned the status of the great hand, a being with an unknown name that was a terrifying omen. I had informed them of the pious nature of that undersea deity. In my own words I read of how it protected the wharf from harm, how the lighthouse was not a lighthouse, but had been a temple to honor that god. It was where, I discovered, the acolytes resided.

I went out to the wharf to ponder at the hand. It had always been there, I had just been blind to it in waking memory, just as I was deaf to the buzz of activity of that esoteric order that made its living in the lighthouse. In my now nightly walks on the wharf, I would spend hours watching the lighthouse come alive with Gregorian chants and phantasmagoric light in unnatural colors. Watching the greenish-purple-orange pulsate with the song summoning that great beast whose hand grappled at my perfect wharf.

Our wedding was held on the wharf, in full view of the lighthouse and with the merciful endorsement of the great deep god. The tips of his fingers seemed closer to breaching the surface, so much so we considered hosting our marriage in the palm of his forbearing hand. Throughout the event I felt the eyes from the lighthouse stabbing through me like the Roman senate cut down Caesar. When I placed the ring on her finger, I felt, for the first time ever on the wharf, unwell.

That night, she talked to me about the lighthouse. Quixotically, I believe it was the first time we had ever truly spoken to each other about the matter. She told me about how she knew the lighthouse, the old one, and the wharf. I asked her what she meant, and she turned away from me. I was left on the wharf that night, with not but the hand of God to stare at. I was alone with nothing but the whole of the wharf, quiet, thoughtful.

The next morning, when I awoke in our apartment, I found our living room destroyed. I knew in a moment she was gone. It devastated me. I found her easel, the only thing untouched, with another perfect painting. The hands of the old god had broken free from the water, one placed on the wharf, another wrapped around the lighthouse. Deep scales, a monochrome black that was almost certainly refined from slime from the sea, covered the burly arms. I saw them flex with vindication, prideful strength that seemed to boast the eldritch nature of the wharf.

I examined the carnage, carnage I knew had always been there. The boats, it seemed, were not a pearly white but rotted. They had collapsed in upon themselves, the wear of time untenably effective in executing those ships. I could only assume that in his emergence, the great one had crushed those boats. I reasoned that there was no need to have such beautiful indulgences as pleasure yachts when the whole of the wharf should be dedicated to the worship of the elder god.

It was after the publication of my second novel that the sense of dread stunned me in permanent stupor. I had long since abandoned our apartment. I needed no home but the wharf, no heat but the breeze that rolled off the sea, no pillow but the inviting grasp of our sacred protector. My books had allowed me to acquire some amount of wealth, but I found that trying to access it twisted my gut into a vile knot. I could not stomach food, save the meager offerings of kelp and raw fish.

It came to pass that I would not sleep. Late in the night on the wharf

I would hear the call of the lost. I often thought I heard her voice in the wind, inviting me to join them deep in the sea. In the frigid winter months, my bones ached for the promised warmth. I would crawl to the edge of the wharf, reaching my fingers towards our benefactor. If there was not a small, fearful part of me, I knew I would not resist his unnatural pull.

During this time, I discovered that many of my fans were coming to this town to see my writings for themselves. They approached me as if I were clad in priestly robes, as if my wild beard was cropped to exude importance. I paid them little mind, except for when they brought me bread or whiskey. I would thank them with prose I had written about our mutual lord, which I had taken to carving into the surface of the wharf itself.

The one time I was able to leave the wharf, I had not slept for days. I stumbled towards our old apartment. I was unsure if it would be inhabited, if it was decimated. My keys failed me, my knock went unanswered. I chose to kick the door in.

Plants I had spent careful summer months cultivating wilted in shattered pots. The smell of coffee had faded, the smell of dust and lost memories remained. A thin film of dirt covered the slashed couch and crushed wooden coffee table in the living room. Still, shockingly, I found scribbled notes and untouched manuscripts describing the great demon below the sea remained unmoved.

On the easel, I saw the wharf crushed, and myself in the carnage. I dared not look out the window, turning to run through the door. He had risen, I knew it. At that moment I also knew that I had invited him. My writing had summoned the Beast of the Bay, and it had doomed our city. Screams from all throughout the town rose in discordant harmony, a cursed chorus for the new god.

His emergence has destroyed the wharf. Warehouses and bars I had rarely acknowledged lay in shambled pieces. Flesh and blood mixed together in a grotesque cabaret, staining what remained of the wood and stone in wild splotches. Although I was mortified, I found my feet moved in curious steps closer to the arisen one. Every step forced me forward, I was caught in mechanical steps toward a being that, dare I set eyes upon it, I knew would drive me to the brink of sanity. His powerful fist pummeled down upon the dock, upon me, and I closed my eyes in anticipation for the impact.

When I opened my eyes, I found the dock calm, the way I had known it in dreams long since passed. The empty whistle of the abandoned town rustled off the shingled homes and sent an ice-cold hand up my spine. The ships rocked silently; the brisk wind nipped at my throat in selfish, ravenous stings. After I absorbed my surroundings, I made the courageous decision to take a step forward. The world did not falter. I blinked. The world did not break.

I was alone, devastatingly alone, except for my wharf. The lighthouse blinked at me, communicating a message I had yet to interpret. I took my seat at a solitary bench, one that I knew well as my bed in months past. The lighthouse still winked toward me while I sat there, seeming to invite me in. I heard, on the wind, as it called my name.

I closed my eyes and opened my ears. The sound of silence made me miss the miserable cries of the seagulls. I thought I could hear her voice. Slowly, I came to the conclusion that it was not sweet mysteries or lascivious offerings, but a request, simple and sincere. I felt compelled, by both the holy bond of matrimony and my natural bond to curiosity, to heed her.

I found that nothing else would dissuade me, so I made my departure from the wharf. My first departure, I found, in a great many years. Her voice promised me that together we could awaken him, bind him to us, and protect our home. I made my way to the lighthouse, certain to answer her call. ♜

≫ CONTRIBUTORS ≪

Jeremiah Dylan Cook is a horror writer whose work has appeared on The NoSleep Podcast, in *Castle of Horror Anthology Volume 4* and *5*, in Ghost Orchid Press's *Hundred Word Horror: Cosmos* and *Beneath* anthologies, and on the Lovecraft eZine's Patreon page. His work has also won first prize in Purple Wall Stories February 2021 Writing Competition, and in the Ligonier Valley Writers 2018 Flash Fiction Contest. In addition, he is a published Lovecraft Scholar with an essay appearing in Hippocampus Press's *Lovecraftian Proceedings No. 4*. While pursuing his bachelor's degree at St. John's University, he received the Mario Mezzacappa Memorial Award for Outstanding Achievement in Poetry and Prose. He completed his master's degree in Writing Popular Fiction at Seton Hill University, and he is a member of the Horror Writers Association. You can learn more about Jeremiah at www.jeremiahdylancook.com, or you can find him on twitter @jeremiahcook1. He is always especially delighted to discuss board games, David Bowie, Tolkien, or Resident Evil video games.

Teel James Glenn's poetry and short stories have been printed in over two hundred magazines including Weird Tales, Mystery Weekly, Pulp Adventures, Space& Time, Mad, Cirsova, Silverblade, and Sherlock Holmes Mystery. His novel *A Cowboy in Carpathia: A Bob Howard Adventure* won best novel 2021 in the Pulp Factory Award. He is also the winner of the 2012 Pulp Ark Award for Best Author. His website is: TheUrbanSwashbuckler.com. Find him on Facebook at Teeljamesglenn and Twitter at @teeljamesglenn.

Liz Holliday has written short stories (the one she's hoping to terrify you with today was in the Stoker winning anthology *Extremes 2: Fantasy and Horror from the Ends of the Earth*; her story *And She Laughed...* was shortlisted for the Crime Writers' Association short story award and adapted for the TV show *The Hunger*), 10 TV novelizations and around 30 books for kids, but she isn't sure she can call herself a writer as she doesn't have a cat.

Most recently she's ventured into screenwriting. Her short film *IRL* is part of the London Screenwriters' Festival anthology feature film The Impact. It will launch later this year, live in London and then online. Find out more at www.impact50film.com.

She currently freelances as a question editor for a mobile trivia games company, where her boss says she ought to have 'Professional Pedant' on her business cards. Liz lives in London (England, not Canada) and you can meet her at www.facebook.com/liz.holliday.39/

P. J. (Tricia) Hoover wanted to be a Jedi, but when that didn't work out, she became an electrical engineer instead. After a fifteen-year bout designing computer chips for a living, P. J. started creating worlds of her own. She's the award-winning author of *The Hidden Code*, a *Da Vinci Code*-style young adult adventure with a kick-butt heroine, and *Tut: The Story of My Immortal Life*, featuring a fourteen-year-old King Tut who's stuck in middle school. When not writing, P. J. spends time practicing kung fu, fixing things around the house, and solving Rubik's cubes. For more information about P. J. (Tricia) Hoover, please visit her website www.pjhoover.com.
Instagram and Twitter: @pj_hoover
Facebook: www.facebook.com/AuthorPJHoover

Steven Philip Jones has written over sixty novels, graphic novels, radio scripts and non-fiction books for adults and young adults. Steven's best-known credits include the graphic novel series *H.P. Lovecraft World*s, the horror-adventure comics series *Nightlinger*, and the review text *The Clive Cussler Adventures: A Critical Review.* A graduate of the University of Iowa, Steven majored in Journalism and Religion and was accepted into Iowa's prestigious Writers' Workshop MFA Program. A proud husband and father, Steven currently resides in northern Utah.

New York Times bestselling author **Alethea Kontis** is a princess, storm chaser, and adventurer. She has written over 20 books and 40 short stories, including *AlphaOops: The Day Z Went First, Enchanted,* and *Prince Phillip's*

Birthday Waltz (Disney). Alethea is the recipient of the Jane Yolen Mid-List Author Grant, the Scribe Award, the Garden State Teen Book Award, and two-time winner of the Gelett Burgess Children's Book Award. She has been twice nominated for both the Andre Norton Nebula and the Dragon Award. Alethea also narrates stories for multiple award-winning online magazines and contributes regular YA book reviews to NPR. Born in Vermont, she currently resides on the Space Coast of Florida with her teddy bear, Charlie. Find out more about Princess Alethea at aletheakontis.com.

Frazer Lee is the author of six novels including Bram Stoker Award®-nominated debut *The Lamplighters*. Winner of the Edgar Allan Poe Gothic Filmmaker Award, Frazer's screenwriting and directing credits include the acclaimed horror films *Panic Button* and *The Stay*. Frazer is Reader in Creative Writing at Brunel University London, and resides with his family in Buckinghamshire, just across the cemetery from the real-life *Hammer House of Horror*. Come break his heart at: www.frazerlee.com.

Will McDermott has published eight novels and 18 short stories, and helped create innumerous worlds, characters, and stories for card, board, and video games. His fiction is often set in gaming universes, including *Magic: The Gathering*, *Warhammer 40K*, and *Mage Wars*. His most recent novel, *Strangled By Death*, is a tale of *Carl Kolchak: The Night Stalker*. Will has written a second *Night Stalker* novel, which should be published in 2022. Find out more at willmcdermott.com. Follow Will on Instagram at @w_mcdermott.

Mike Owsley is a political operative, activist, and author. He enjoys suddenly moving to new places, reading, and drinking coffee (which he does in unimaginable, and medically inadvisable, quantities). You can follow him @BigMikeOwsley on Twitter or look at his website MikeOwsley.com, both of which are also not medically advised.

Scott Pearson is a full-time freelance writer and editor. He has published across a number of genres, such as literary fiction, mystery, urban fantasy, horror, and science fiction, including three *Star Trek* stories and two *Trek* novellas. His essay "Baby, Please Don't Go" appeared in *Outside in Wants to Believe: 156 New Perspectives on 156 X-Files Universe Stories*. His stories "The Ghosts of Glenmirror" and "The Murder Couple" appeared in *Castle of Horror 4* and *5*, respectively. He co-developed, with William Leisner, *Tales of the Weird World War*, an alternate history/horror/sci-fi series which debuted in 2021 with the short novels *The Big Dark & Meet John Doe*; "The Loneliness of Monsters" takes place several years later in that same world. Scott lives in personable St. Paul, Minnesota, with his wife, Sandra, and their cat, Ripley. He and his daughter, Ella, cohost the podcast *Generations Geek*. Visit Scott online at scott-pearson.com and generationsgeek.com and follow him on Twitter @smichaelpearson.

Tom Waltz is the Group Editor/Creative Development for premiere comic book publisher IDW Publishing, as well as the writer of numerous critically acclaimed graphic novels, including *Teenage Mutant Ninja Turtles*, *The Last Fall*, *Children of the Grave*, *After the Fire*, amongst others. A former U.S. Marine and Desert Storm vet, he grew up in Clinton, Michigan and currently makes his home in San Diego, California.

Lewis Figun Westbrook (he/they) is a comedian first as it is a defense mechanism appropriate for any setting, and a writer second as it is a defense mechanism best saved for time alone in a room where they can cry all they want. They love puns, pretending they can do sports, and talking to people. Even though all of those things make them nervous. Find them on most social media @lewisrllw.

CASTLE BRIDGE MEDIA RECOMMENDS...

If you liked *The Castle of Horror Anthology Volume 7: Love Gone Wrong*, you might also enjoy reading the following titles from Castle Bridge Media available on Amazon or by order at your favorite book store:

Austinites
By In Churl Yo

Bloodsucker City
By Jim Towns

THE CASTLE OF HORROR
ANTHOLOGY SERIES
Volume 1
Volume 2: *Holiday Horrors*
Volume 3: *Scary Summer Stories*
Volume 4: *Women Running From Houses*
Volume 5: *Thinly Veiled: The 70s*
Volume 6: *Femme Fatales**
Volume 7: *Love Gone Wrong*
Edited By Jason Henderson and In Churl Yo
*Edited By P.J. Hoover

Castle of Horror Podcast
Book of Great Horror:
Our Favorites, Top Tens
and Bizarre Pleasures
Edited By Jason Henderson

FuturePast Sci-Fi Anthology
Edited by In Churl Yo

Isonation
By In Churl Yo

MID-LIFE CRISIS THRILLERS
18 Miles From Town
By Jason Henderson

THE PATH
The Blue-Spangled Blue
By David Bowles
The Deepest Green
By David Bowles

SURF MYSTIC
Night of the Book Man
By Peyton Douglas

Nightwalkers: Gothic Horror Movies
By Bruce Lanier Wright

Please remember to leave us your reviews on Amazon and Goodreads!

THANK YOU FOR SUPPORTING INDEPENDENT PUBLISHERS AND AUTHORS!

castlebridgemedia.com